HER UNDENIABLE DISTRACTION

WOMEN OF PARK MANOR

SHERELLE GREEN

ROSE GOLD PRESS, LLC

Rose Gold Press, LLC

Chicago, Illinois

www.RoseGoldPress.com

Editor: Nicole Falls

Cover Design: Sherelle Green

*To my lit sisters, Angela Seals, Anita Davis, Elle Wright, &
Sheryl Lister, the paths we took to get here may have been different,
however, we were led to this destination together. I value our talks,
our dreams, our conversations… Thank you for being the amazing
women you are!*

DEAR READER

Are you a believer in fate or do you believe we control our own destiny? I remember asking that question to my family and friends before and the answers I received were all across the board. In Her Undeniable Distraction, fate is a key element of discussion and you'll see how when you join Burgundy and Kane on their journey.

I have to say, Burgundy and Kane turned out differently than I'd originally planned, yet sometimes, the characters demand to re-write their own stories and there is nothing we can do about it but let them live. In the end, I learned that the theme of the book affected me in ways I hadn't even realized. Ironic that I had a plan that morphed into something different. Fate, maybe?

I also invite you to read the excerpt in the back of this book for Fake News. It's part of my social experiment series, but can be read as a stand-alone (hero and heroine were never introduced before). I shared this excerpt because fate also played a starring role. If you're already read it, then you know I mean. If you haven't, check it out :).

HER UNDENIABLE DISTRACTION

Burgundy Anderson has always loved helping people. So naturally, there's nothing this Leasing Manager wouldn't do for the Santa Monica residents of Park Manor. Problem is, this workaholic needs a life outside of the lavish establishment and if she's going to leave her mark in the world, she'll need to figure out her next step with no distractions. Insert Kane Brooks, otherwise known as, the delicious distraction determined to make his presence known.

Landscape Artist Kane Brooks is a glass half full type of man. Things happen for a reason and when he runs across the sassy woman with a cause, he's knows the stars have aligned, leading his thoughts straight to the bedroom. Their kisses are as sexy as she is, but he can't seem to get her to sit still long enough for a repeat performance. When fate gives him a second chance, he snatches at the opportunity. She may think she can run, but he's always considered himself a track star.

PROLOGUE

Burgundy

I never liked Buddy's shady ass. Yet, here I was, sitting in Park Manor Tavern at his memorial service pretending to care about the fact that he was gone. It wasn't that I was a heartless bitch. In fact, sometimes I thought I cared too deeply about unimportant shit.

Growing up, my mama would always tell me that caring too much about folks would get me in trouble one day. She said the key to a happy life was to look out for yourself and no one else. She wasn't the best mom, but she was all I'd had before she'd passed, so I took everything she'd said to heart. Still did.

If my mama would have ever met Buddy there was no doubt in my mind she would have felt the same way I felt about him. I always had an issue with people who weren't being real or acting like their true self. Buddy always seemed sneaky, like he was up to no good. At least he seemed that way to me.

He was hired as the bellman way before I'd become the leasing manager of Park Manor, a luxury condo community. Therefore, I had to deal with him from jump. To me, his eyes always seemed a little shifty. Kinda like the type that would rob you in your sleep, so I never understood how he'd gotten a job that literally meant he got to see everyone walk in and out of their home.

I'd always been able to spot bullshit a mile away and Buddy might as well had been walking around wearing a white t-shirt with bright ass red letters that said *I was looking for my knife. I think I left it in your back.*

And why did no one ever question how close he was to Hazel, a Park Manor resident? Word was, Hazel's family had that old California money and when Buddy wasn't doing his job, he was all up in Hazel's condo making up some shit as to why he had to go up there.

No ma'am. Something wasn't right about their relationship. Buddy had one too many skeletons in his closet that had come to light but never been addressed. So for the most part, I'd steered clear of him as much as I could.

Yet to be fair, Buddy wasn't the only shady person I'd come across working at Park Manor, which was insane because you'd think luxury places would only come with rich folks' problems. There was this one time that they hired a barista for the café we had in the lobby who we found out was pocketing thousands of dollars over the course of the few months he worked here. His name was Manny or something like that. Only thing I didn't understand was why management and security didn't notice the money missing until homeboy slipped up and told his girl who ratted his ass out.

Then there was this other time that they hired a woman who called herself Candy. Within minutes of interviewing for an office assistant role in the leasing department, she had all of the dumbass men I worked with eating out the palm of her hand. I didn't trust her from day one, so imagine my not-so-surprised face when the property manager told me that they'd caught Candy having sex in the office.

Turns out, she often lured male visitors of Park Manor into the office after hours to participate in some extra-curricular activities in exchange for some cash. I'd just so happened to be in the office the morning they let her go. So when my asshole boss told me not to say anything to Candy as security packed up her things and escorted her out, I of course, didn't listen and asked her how much she'd made during her time working here out of curiosity. She hadn't told me, but my guess based off the conversations I'd overheard? Ms. Candy had made enough to buy a damn candy store.

So, I guess one could say I'd seen a lot of shit in the years I'd worked here and had to put up with even more crap from the few residents who thought their shit didn't stink. But I had to remain neutral in my position. Case in point, it would have looked terrible if I hadn't showed up to Buddy's memorial despite how much I'd rather be getting ten painful Brazilian waxes after a shave day than be in this establishment right now.

Crazy thing was, I could look around the bar and tell that some folks were genuinely gonna miss Buddy. Older men were lifting shots into the air before downing the liquid. Older women were shaking their head and patting one another on the hand for comfort. Some young dudes were sharing stories about how Buddy was always down to shoot the shit with them. Yet, out of all the people mourning his death, the ones who surprised me the most were the women around my age who were dabbing their eyes in sorrow.

Honestly, from what I could tell, a few of them were really hurt by his death. Observing them made me feel like I was truly a fraud for being here. *As if I didn't feel that way enough sometimes.* Regardless of its faults, I loved Park Manor. It was home. My home.

"Another whiskey sour?" the bartender asked. I almost declined another drink, but then I figured another taste of good ol' Jack Daniels would do me some good. He was the type of man I could kick it with after a long day. He could be bitter, but he never complained. Never talked back. Ending a night with him meant some of the best sleep of my life. And even if he made me question my deep throating abilities at times, eventually, he always went down smooth.

"Okay, where to sit," I said aloud, glancing at the tables around the packed bar.

"The host can tell you where you're sitting," the bartender said, overhearing me.

"I'm sorry, what?"

"The host has everyone's assigned seat." He nodded toward the woman standing at the door. "We knew it would be packed for Buddy, so we thought assigning seats would be best."

I forced a smile and excused myself so I could get my assigned seat. If I hadn't just gotten a fresh sip of my dude Jack, there was no way in hell I'd be staying. *Who assigns seats at a bar anyway?* Even in death, Buddy was working my last nerve.

After I got my assigned seat, I made my way to the circular mahogany booth that sat in the corner of the bar, grateful that I'd at least been assigned a decent seat.

"Ladies, glad to see I was paired with great table-mates," I announced as I approached the table.

"I thought the same thing," Teegan said, followed by similar sentiments from Kathi, and Paityn. All three women were Park Manor residents and women who I was glad I had the pleasure to know. Being that I not only lived at Park Manor, but also worked here, I pretty much knew everyone. Yet, I had to admit that I didn't hang out with my neighbors nearly as much as I could have.

I guess you could say all work and no play made Burgundy a boring ass bitch because there was no reason that I should be so hyped to catch up with women I could see anytime I pleased. Granted, some had lived at Park Manor longer than others, some had more money while others were maxing out their savings account *cough* *raises hand *cough*, and we definitely didn't all have the same living quarters, yet, we were connected in some way. There was beauty in being a Parky, as I liked to call us.

The last one to join our table group was one of the newest Park Manor residents, Skylar. I could immediately tell that something was going on with her and my gut was telling me that it was something serious. I always hated to see people suffer, especially when I didn't know them well enough to help them. Even so, Skylar seemed like she needed a lifeline and her eyes were so sad, it broke my heart. I made a mental note right then and there to put more of an effort forth with this new Parky and see if the warning signs I sensed were accurate.

As conversation flowed, I was reminded of how much I loved the residents. In their own way, these women were doin' their thang and I realized that I needed to make more of an effort to not be the same ol' Burgundy I always was.

Sitting there, sipping cocktails and laughing with them as memories about Buddy and others were shared around the table, I made it a point to do better at putting myself out there with folks. If I was gonna take away anything from Buddy's memorial, it was that life was short and you could drop dead without a moment's notice.

I wasn't even tryin' to be insincere. Just honest. And despite how I felt about Buddy, it was clear that he'd impacted a lot of people. Left a legacy in his own way. I'd already seen a lot of death at my young age and each and every time, I asked myself the same question. *What legacy will I leave behind?*

My mama hadn't left a great one, and granted, being the hilarious local alcoholic that could always make folks laugh wasn't what she probably set out to be, but she'd still left a legacy. Yet for me, I was still trying to figure my shit out. Folks were either going to like you or hate you. I hated that in-between, grey area shit. If I was going to leave my impact on the world, I needed to craft a plan that made sense. A plan that said *Burgundy is that bitch, if you don't know her, you need to.* And maybe, just maybe, my love for Park Manor would help me get there.

CHAPTER 1

Burgundy

 *ix months later…*

"This must be a damn joke," I hollered.

"Language," Larry, the property manager of Park Manor, said.

"My bad." I cleared my throat. "This must be a *fucking* joke," I said louder, completely baffled by the situation before me.

"Burgundy, no matter how upset you are, I won't tolerate that kind of language in my office."

I huffed, refusing to apologize. "You're really firing me?" I asked. "After everything I've done for Park Manor and the residents here, you're letting me go without a moment's notice?"

I started pacing the small confines of his office with walls so brown, it always made me think of a toilet of poop. When we'd been choosing colors for the office revamp a couple years ago, Larry had been all too eager to choose the kind of brown that was slightly more yellowish than the milky Hershey color. Which meant, he'd painted his entire office to look like runny shit. Literally.

I couldn't believe I'd worked for a dumbass like Larry for so long just like I couldn't believe what he was saying to me right now. And the fact that he was giving me this bad news on my six-year anniversary of being a leasing manager for Park Manor was beyond messed up.

"Think of this as a fresh start for you to do something that better suits you," he said.

Who the hell is he to tell me what suits me? I was boiling, but couldn't even think straight when he followed up his comment by saying, "Trust me, this is harder for me than it is for you."

"I highly doubt that," I told him. I was trying to control my frustration, but I was doing a terrible job. Losing my job had been the last thought on my mind today.

"You'll get a nice severance package," he informed me.

I shook my head. "It's a shitty severance package. Candy got offered more when you fired her."

"This situation is a little more serious." Larry leaned back in his desk chair with a smug look on his face.

"Right. I can totally see how checking the little box that stated my highest degree earned was a bachelor's degree as opposed to high school is worse than having sex with numerous men in the office."

"Exactly," he said with a nod. "Glad you see my point."

Was this fool serious? "No Larry. I don't see your point. This is unfair on so many levels."

I knew what he saw when he looked at me. He saw a young, uneducated Black woman who hadn't gotten her degree, but was the most well-liked employee in Park Manor's leasing office. I wasn't refined to his standards. Far from it. Yet, I was intelligent and knew how to play the game and I played it damn well.

When he'd initially hired me six years ago, I was sure it was to fulfill a quota since management had informed him that they needed at least one person of color in the office. He hadn't expected me to slay my job and increase the number of happy residents to figures they'd never seen before.

I knew my shit and I was good at what I did. I was also a bit of a workaholic and poured everything I had into Park Manor. We didn't win best complex on the block year after year by coincidence.

"It's not unfair," he said. "You and I both know that you lied about a few more things on your application as well, but I'll do you a favor and not mention those aloud since I'm sure some of your colleagues are listening."

I clenched my jaw because yeah, I was sure the good ol' boys club was listening to every word that Larry was saying and enjoying the fact that I was getting let go.

"Oh, and I'll need you out by the end of the day."

Of course you do. "I never kept many personal items at this job anyway," I told him.

"That may be true, but there's a lot of items in your apartment."

I froze. "Wait, what? I don't understand."

Larry gave me another stupid, smug smile. "You were offered discounted rent by being the leasing manager on property. However, now that you are no longer employed here, we'll need you out of your apartment by the end of the day."

"You've got to be shitting me!"

"I shit you not," he taunted, sounding like a proper asshole.

"Where am I supposed to go?" I asked. "Kicking me out by the end of the day is insane! I can't pack everything that fast!"

"We'll help you," Larry said. "I've already informed the guys that we'll be doing a group activity this evening."

What the fuck? Having any one of them touch my personal things would be an absolute nightmare. "No, I don't want any of your help. This has to be illegal."

Larry handed me a packet of paper stapled in the corner. "It's absolutely legal. When you first started working here, you signed the contract stating that you'd vacate the premises – office and apartment – within twenty-four hours if let go."

Rolling my eyes, I reminded him that, "Twenty-four hours is not by the end of the day Larry."

He rubbed his chin. "Hmm. I guess you're right. Tell you what. Since I'm feeling so generous, you have until tomorrow evening to be out of your apartment."

"How kind of you," I voiced dryly. Not wanting to give him a chance to say anything else to me, I walked out of his office briefly noticing my ex-colleagues tiptoeing back to their desks.

I was able to drop all of the personal items on my desk into a box in one swoop of my right arm. As I walked out of the leasing office, I briefly glanced each way down the hall to make sure I didn't run into any residents. The last thing I wanted was for someone to ask me what was in the box. Or worse, force me to participate in small talk as if they couldn't tell I had real life shit going on.

I stumbled into my apartment, on the verge of tears, but refusing to let myself cry over this mess. It wasn't the first setback that I'd ever faced, but I had to admit, I was embarrassed about it. News traveled fast in Park Manor and it was only a matter of time before everyone in the community knew that I was let go.

A part of me knew I should call the residents who I was friends with – Teegan, Skylar, Kathi, and Paityn. I'd been growing closer to each of the ladies after the memorial and I was sure they would be just as pissed as I was to learn what had happened. Yet, as I pulled out my phone, I couldn't even bring myself to dial any of their numbers.

Crap. And I just gave my aunt all that money. My aunt had practically raised me and being that we were extremely close, I hadn't hesitated to wipe out my savings to help her pay for some renovations of her home knowing I'd make it back after a couple paychecks. After giving her the money, I'd paid off my credit cards and that expensive ass solo trip I'd gone on. *What am I going to do?* Better yet, where was I going to stay? I hadn't stayed with my aunt in years, but I was sure she'd welcome me back with open arms.

I glanced around my apartment, still in a bit of shock about everything that had occurred today. I'd hit an all-time low and to make matters worse, I couldn't even afford to sleep off my sorrows because I had to pack up all my shit. The place had come furnished, but I had a lot of my own things to pack up. So, I grabbed some boxes from the building's mailing room and got to work. Twenty-four hours or not, I wanted to leave this place as soon as possible and buy myself some time before I faced my friends and the other residents.

* * *

"AND, THAT'S THE LAST ONE," I muttered. Nine hours later, I was completely packed up and had convinced Norman, one of the new bellmen, to let me store some items in a storage locker and keep it on the low until I could pick everything up in a couple days. Like a thief in the night, I snuck out of the back door of Park Manor around four in the morning, pushing two large carts of boxed items and dragging those carts two blocks down to avoid any residents on morning runs. Did I care that I had to leave those carts on the sidewalk? Not really. Park Manor had plenty of them.

Overall, I was being a little extra, but I didn't care. It also wasn't typical to order an Uber to move out of your apartment versus renting a truck, but I needed to save all my pennies right now and I didn't own a car. Never needed one.

Standing on the sidewalk, I said a silent prayer when my phone notified me that my Uber driver would pick me up in five minutes. A smile crossed my lips when I noticed that my driver was Maurice, a dude that seemed to always be the Uber driver in the area. He loved to hear the sound of his own voice and was annoying as hell, but homeboy was a loyal as they came. If there was anything he saw or something you did that you shouldn't have, Mo wasn't saying shit. Which meant, I could trust him not to mention anything about picking me up in his SUV with two carts of my belongings. Plus, any other driver would see me and keep driving.

Not only did I have a lot of shit with me, but I was also wearing some pink and yellow Sailor Moon pajama bottoms with the matching hoodie – attire that was a couple sizes too small and inappropriate for several reasons. However, I'd had the pajamas since high school and I always wore them when I needed to feel better about a messed-up situation. *Plus, at least the weather is warm.* I'd be freezing my ass off if it was ten degrees cooler. California weather was great overall, but the fall was always a little chilly for my taste.

Mo's black SUV pulled up right on time and I breathed a sigh of relief that I was going to be away from any nosy eyes soon. The window didn't roll down right away and the fact that Mo hadn't addressed me yet made me nervous, so I double checked the license plate. Concluding it was indeed Mo's truck, I waved, but didn't step closer to the car.

The rest seemed to happen in slow motion as the driver stepped out of the vehicle and walked over to where I was standing on the sidewalk. *What the...* Nothing made sense in that moment and I was frozen in place at the sight of the amused dark brown eyes looking my way.

"Burgundy, I'd hoped that was you on the app."

"Uh." I opened my mouth to speak, but my tongue was held hostage, sticking to the floor of my mouth as if it were magnetic.

"It's me," he said in that husky voice I'd dreamt

about a lot lately despite my best efforts to think about anything else. *Anyone* else.

"Yeah, I can see it's you," I responded, finding my voice. Albeit, it was a rude voice, but I'd found it none-theless.

"Damn." He placed his hand over his chest. "I thought you'd be happier to see me."

I frowned. "What I don't understand is why you're the one picking me up. You're not Maurice."

He shook his head and laughed. "Nah. Maurice got held up and asked me to take a couple of his rides. I'm his cousin." He stepped a little closer to me causing me to run into one of the carts. "Imagine my surprise when your name popped up as my next pick up. I was just about to clock out for the night."

"It's morning," I corrected.

He shrugged. "That's a matter of opinion. I've been taking rides all night." His eyes looked me up and down, that stupid smirk curling even more as he read aloud the words on my pajamas.

"Sailor Jupiter was always my favorite. Underrated if you ask me."

I smacked my lips. "Boy, don't pretend like you watched Sailor Moon."

"Considering I'm the youngest of three and my older siblings are women, then yeah, I know all about it." He took another step toward me. "And since it looks like you've had a shitty twenty-four hours, I'll let that *boy* comment slide." His eyes landed on the only freckles I had on my entire body that were located on my right cheek. When he reached up to gently touch them, I was surprised that I didn't flinch, but instead, welcomed his warmth. "Or did you forget that I'm all man."

14

"I don't know what you mean," I said quickly, taking a step back. "And I have some real-life shit going on, so right now I'm kinda shocked that you're here."

He glanced to the carts of boxes. "You want to tell me why it looks like you're moving in the middle of the night?"

"More like early morning," I corrected again. "And no, I don't really want to explain. If Mo were here, he wouldn't question me, so are you gonna help me load up the truck or keep asking questions I won't answer?"

He held up his hands in defeat. "Okay, I can take a hint." Without asking me any more questions, he began loading the truck. A part of me was worried that something wouldn't fit and I'd have to sneak it back into the storage locker I was borrowing at Park Manor, but he made everything fit and looked effortless doing it.

I thought he'd remain quiet the entire drive, but once we hit a little traffic, he broke the silence. "So, you're headed to Crenshaw?"

"Yeah," I answered, although I shouldn't have had to. He had the address in his Uber app already.

"Are you visiting your aunt for a while?"

"You know, I distinctly remember saying we wouldn't share any details about our life with one another other than our names."

He laughed. "That was before you got drunk that one time and blurted out that your aunt lived in Crenshaw and made the best caramel cake in the world."

Ugh. I knew better than to drink around strangers. "Do you hear how creepy this conversation sounds or is this the way you are with all your Uber customers?"

"Believe it or not, I didn't talk to any of those drunk ass folks I picked up," he stated. "And I told Mo this is the first and last time I'll be helping him out, so I don't know proper Uber etiquette. He could get in trouble for this shit."

"You're right, he could." I pulled out my phone knowing good and well he was looking at me in the rearview mirror. "Maybe I should file a complaint that the man who picked me up is not the man in the photo for the Uber I reserved."

He shook his head. "Only if you want Mo to lose his job." My eyes caught his in the mirror. "But I think you're bluffin', so I'll take my chances and ask you one more question."

"That I may or may not answer."

"Why do you have so much stuff with you?" he asked. "Is everything okay?"

I sighed. "Short answer? No, I'm not okay. As for the long version, like I mentioned before, I'd rather not talk about it."

Luckily, he didn't push me for more details and twenty minutes later, we were at my aunt's.

"We can just unload everything onto the porch," I told him after we both got out of the car. I knew my aunt wasn't home since she started working early in the morning, but I had my own key.

"Are you moving everything inside?" he asked after I'd opened the front door.

"Yeah, but it's cool, I got it. The porch is fine for now."

I was sure he'd heard me loud and clear, but then I noticed he was actually placing the boxes he'd unloaded already into the foyer.

"I told you, the porch is fine," I reminded him.

"I heard you, but this is a lot to move and you don't

want this stuff just out here on the porch for anyone to snatch."

"I know most of the neighbors," I explained. "It will be fine."

"Let me help you."

"I got it," I repeated, my voice growing slightly louder than I'd anticipated. "Why won't you take a damn hint already?"

He placed the box in his hands down. "So, let me get this straight. I was good enough to pick you up on the sidewalk and load all this stuff into the SUV. But I'm not good enough to go into your aunt's house?"

Sighing, I briefly closed my eyes hoping he'd go away. He didn't. "Just leave me alone. I appreciate all of your help this morning, but I don't have time for this." The tone in my voice was a mix of frustration and annoyance. A bad combination for an Anderson woman.

"Wow," he said. "Would it kill you to let your guard down long enough to let someone actually be there for you?"

I rolled my eyes. "You don't know me. Not really. And the brief time we spent together hardly qualifies you as someone to question how often I let my guard down."

He mumbled something under his breath that I couldn't quite make out, so I called him out on it.

Shaking his head, he told me, "You don't want to know what I was thinking," before gently grabbing my hand and tugging me toward him.

My heart was beating so fast, it was hard to catch my breath. But he didn't seem to care about the effect he was having on me. When we'd first met, I'd been in a different place. I'd just come to the realization that I needed to be a better version of myself. I'd had a great job with amazing pay. I'd decided to open myself up to new friendships. And I'd been ready to embark on the journey of a lifetime. Yet now? Now, all of that seemed like ancient history. Broke, evicted, and pissed as hell, I wasn't the Burgundy he'd met months ago, but rather, a bootlegged version of myself.

Yet, the way he was looking at me made me feel like he saw something I didn't. "You know, if it weren't for the way your breath seems to catch when I get close to you, I'd swear you'd forgotten all about the time we shared together." His voice was lower. Softer.

My eyes went to his lips despite my internal warning to myself. They looked so soft. So kissable. And just like I'd remembered. Which meant, I didn't have time to entertain whatever he was laying down right now.

"The time we shared was cool, but not too memorable," I lied. "Honestly, I wouldn't have given you a second thought had you not shown up in Mo's SUV."

He held my gaze. "So, you've forgotten all about me, huh?"

"Yep. Erased from my memory."

He squinted, observing me; his eyes a mixture of annoyance and amusement. "Is that so?" he asked.

"Afraid it is." My voice sounded a little shaky, but I kept my head held high. Forget meeting him? *Ha!* As if I could ever forget meeting Kane Brooks.

CHAPTER 2

*I*celand: Day One…
         (five months ago)

Burgundy

"I'M NOT sure this was the best idea," I mumbled to myself as I thought about the trek I'd made through Keflavik International Airport. Leave it to me to decide that the best way to get boring Burgundy out of her shell was to fly solo to Iceland for a ten-day tour.

It had been a month since Buddy's memorial, which marked the day I'd decided to really focus on building my legacy. Although the tour company had boasted about it being safe and highly recommended, it didn't stop me from wondering what the hell I'd been thinking when I brought the Groupon for this getaway.

The sixteen hours it had taken me to get here hadn't helped my attitude since my layover in Finland was supposed to have been at least three hours, yet, I'd found myself racing through the airport to make my connecting flight after my plane out of Los Angeles was stuck on the runway for three hours.

And now, I was standing in line at the American Airlines desk after watching the baggage go around for the eleventh time and not seeing my suitcase. Luckily, the line went fast and I was to the front in no time. Yet, after giving them my information and the employee doing a quick search, they voiced the words I dreaded hearing.

"What do you mean, you've lost my bags?"

"We're sorry ma'am," the desk attendant stated looking anything but sorry. "However, if you fill out the claim form, we'll do our best to deliver your suitcase to your hotel when it arrives."

Grinding my teeth, I counted to ten in an attempt to calm my nerves. "The main problem with that is the fact that I will only be in this first hotel for two nights. I'm on a tour and will be in several different locations while I'm here."

She continued to type in whatever she was so focused on as she basically repeated her words. After a couple more minutes, I gave up and filled out the claim form before pulling out my phone to check the email I'd been sent with directions on where to go for pick up.

I frustratingly made my way to the baggage claim exit doors, grateful that I had at least packed two outfits and underwear into my carry-on suitcase. Deciding I needed to make a detour to the bathroom first, I took a sharp right, running right into someone who had been turning that same corner.

"Shit," I huffed, immediately dropping to pick up my belongings that had fallen out of my purse.

"Sorry about that," someone said kneeling beside me. His voice was deep and kinda gruff like he'd been rushing through baggage claim or talking on the phone. When I glanced up, I half expected to find him as annoyed as I was, but he looked just the opposite. His eyes were playful and welcoming and his teeth had to be some of the straightest and whitest teeth I'd ever seen before.

After we'd picked up everything in my purse, I opened my mouth to tell him he didn't need to apologize since it was my fault, but I couldn't find my voice. *Damn.* My last boyfriend had been more of a redbone pretty boy, but Mr. Baggage Claim was the complete opposite. Dark brown skin. Full beard. A head of hair and a wave game that made me wonder if he still wore a durag. He'd only said three words, but he sounded American when he'd said them.

He was tall too. Much taller than me and I was almost five ten. But I couldn't even focus on checking him out and not get hung up on his lips. I was a sucker for a good pair of lips and his were firm, yet juicy. I bet every woman who'd ever kissed him nibbled on his lips for a while, unable to help themselves.

"I'm the one who should be sorry," I finally voiced. "It's been a rough start to my trip and I wasn't watching where I was going."

"If it's already going shitty, it can only get better, right?" he asked.

I squinted, a little confused by his comment. "No, it could definitely get worse. Even when things are already bad, there is no rule saying that the bad shit that has happened in one day won't reach another level of frustration."

His dark brown eyes held mine as he explained, "But if it weren't for bad shit happening, how would we know when we're due for something good in our life? Wouldn't you say that the good stuff is so much sweeter after dealing with a chain of unpredictable bullshit?"

His logic wasn't my cup of tea, but I couldn't argue that he didn't have a point. Still, something wouldn't let me give him the satisfaction. "Well, as enlightening as this conversation is, I should be going."

"Me too," he said. For a brief moment, he looked like wanted to say more, but he didn't. We walked away in the directions we were previously headed, neither of us making an effort to even share our names.

The bathroom line was long as it usually seemed for women's restrooms. I couldn't stop thinking about the conversation I'd had with the sexy stranger and was still thinking about him as I followed the signs to the shuttle pick up, grateful to find the white bus with teal lettering for my tour group right away.

"What's your name please?" a woman asked, holding a clipboard. Her Icelandic accent was thick, but her English was clear.

"Burgundy Anderson."

"Ah, yes. Ms. Anderson. Here you are. You're one of the last to arrive for the first shuttle bus." She checked off the box by my name before glancing around at my feet. "Is that your only luggage?"

"My main suitcase was lost, but I gave them the address to the first hotel."

"As stated in your itinerary, we are going to the second location after two nights. If you have your claim form, I'll get one of the assistants in the office to keep your airline abreast of our itinerary."

My eyes widened in delighted surprise. "Oh my goodness, that would be amazing! I was thinking I'd have to do the rest of this tour naked."

The sound of a someone chuckling caused me to glance behind me at the eavesdropper. "I should have known," I said, shaking my head. "So we meet again Mr. Baggage Claim."

He laughed louder. "Is that who I am? Mr. Baggage Claim?"

I shrugged. "The nickname fits, don't you think?"

"I guess." His eyes made a slow perusal of me in a way he hadn't when we'd run into each other earlier. Extending his hand, he introduced himself. "You can call me Mr. Baggage Claim, or if you prefer, my name is Kane."

"Burgundy." I accepted his hand, refusing to think about his previous words because surprisingly, he was right. After the shitty flight I'd had and losing my luggage, the day was already getting better. "Did I forget to pick up something off the floor?"

"Nah, you didn't overlook anything," he said before nodding at the shuttle bus. "It seems we're on the same tour."

"No we're not," I spurted, which was stupid considering who was I to tell him that he wasn't on the same tour as me. "I mean, is that so?"

"Yeah," he chuckled before the lady with the clipboard checked him in and told us we could be seated on the bus. I tried not to focus on the fact that he was standing so close behind me, I could smell his earthy cologne as it seductively teased my nostrils.

"It's pretty crowded," he whispered. "But there's two seats four rows back."

Of course there are. It wasn't that I didn't want to sit next to him that made me walk slowly to the only empty seats on the bus. It was the fact that there was no way I could be at ease sitting next to a man who looked as sexy as he did. My only hope was that the drive wouldn't be that long.

"Okay folks," the tour guide announced. "Get settled and make sure you have your cameras ready to capture the scenery. We're taking you on the scenic route, so we'll be arriving at the first hotel in about two hours. Later tonight, the second shuttle bus will join us at the hotel for passengers arriving later."

"Two hours?" I mumbled. *Shit.* That meant one-hundred and twenty minutes of squeezing my thighs together, ignoring the fact that I hadn't been this close to an attractive man in longer than I cared to admit.

"If you get tired," he murmured, "you can place your head on my shoulder to get comfortable."

I smiled, settling into my window seat. "Thanks, but that won't be necessary."

He laughed which seemed to be what he liked to do most around me. "If you say so. Just know the offer stands if you change your mind."

"I won't," I responded. There was no way I was going to lay on his shoulder to get comfortable. I was never the PDA type of woman and I hadn't even done that mushy stuff when I was in a serious relationship.

Yet, to my surprise, as we cruised along that beautiful Icelandic road, my eyes grew tired and I found my head drifting to the right, bumping into something firm and strong. It wasn't until we arrived at the hotel that I realized Kane was the reason I'd experienced the best nap I'd ever had.

CHAPTER 3

Kane

Erased from her memory? I'd known Burgundy Anderson was a tough nut to crack when I first met her, but today, she was being extra difficult. My gut was telling me she was bluffing and hadn't forgotten me like she stated. Lord knows I hadn't forgotten her.

She was puckering her lips in a way that I'd grown to miss. We'd only spent ten days together, but they'd been ten days that were etched forever in my memory. Times I didn't think I'd forget anytime soon.

I wanted to console her, I just wasn't sure what for. Her words may have been warning me to leave her the hell alone, but her eyes were painting a different story. When we'd met months ago, she'd seemed so full of life and excited for some revelations she'd had about her life. Yet now, today, she seemed so defeated.

"I'm sorry," I told her, sitting on the top stair of her aunt's porch and motioning for her to take a seat.

"What are you sorry for?" she asked, sitting beside me. "For being annoying or for being nosy?"

"I'm apologizing for the question I'm about to ask again." She looked like she wanted to respond, so I pushed on. "What happened today?" I asked, although I knew I should just drop it. I couldn't help myself. She seemed so upset and there had to be a logical reason why she'd been waiting on the sidewalk with two carts of her stuff.

"I was fired today," she blurted, catching me off guard. "I am – or I mean, I was – a leasing manager for Park Manor, the luxury condo community in Santa Monica. You picked me up two blocks from there. Since I was also living on the premises, I was also evicted yesterday too. Spent all night packing my shit up."

Damn. A part of me was regretful I'd asked since her feelings about her situation were still so raw. "I'm sorry that happened to you," I told her. "I didn't know what you did for a living, but I remember you telling me how much you loved your job."

She dropped her head into her hands. "Honestly, I still can't believe it. I haven't even brought myself to tell anyone else yet. I figured I'd call and tell my aunt after I brought my stuff inside."

Sliding closer, I took a chance and gently touched her shoulder. "You've had a rough twenty-four hours. At least let me help you bring everything inside."

Her mouth turned to the side and she seemed to contemplate my offer. After a few seconds of silence, she finally gave in and let me help her bring her belongings into her aunt's home. It didn't take long with the two of us and several times, I had to stop myself from asking her any more questions that would make her uncomfortable.

When we reached the last couple boxes, I felt a need to be honest with her about something that had been on my mind since she told me her bad news, but she stopped me.

"Actually, hold that thought," she said, looking from me to the open front door. "Would you maybe want to come inside for a cup of coffee or something? I could use the company after the day I've had."

I knew what I should have said, but I wanted to play with her a little. "I can come in under one condition?"

She lifted an eyebrow. "And what's that?"

Looking her up and down, I made sure she knew I was dead serious when I told her, "I'll stay for coffee if you admit that there's no way you forgot about the time we shared together."

She shrugged. "Well, I guess that means you won't be having any coffee this morning. At least not with me."

"Guess so." I dropped off the last box and began my descent down the stairs. "I wish you the best of luck, Burgundy. And I think this is only a minor setback for you. You'll be back on your feet in no time."

"That's it?" she asked when I'd reached the bottom of the stairs.

"What do you mean?"

"Just because I won't admit to anything, you're leaving?"

"Seems that way," I yelled behind me, even though I really did want to stay and have that coffee she'd offered. "I'll catch you around, Burgundy."

"You don't even have my number," she said.

Glancing over my shoulder, I asked, "Are you gonna give it to me?"

"How about you give me yours and I'll text you?" she suggested.

I rattled off my number before heading back to Mo's SUV. Leaving her on the porch was one of the toughest things I'd done all week because every bone in my body was telling me to go back to her and see if staying for coffee really meant something a lot more intimate.

She may have been surprised to see me today, but I hadn't been all that surprised to see her. Southern California wasn't as big as some people thought and I was a firm believer in fate bringing two people together no matter the distance or time. Which meant, if fate was on my side, Ms. Anderson was going to see me again whether she liked it or not.

"Yo, Mo, you here?" I yelled when I got to my cousin's apartment.

"I'm in the kitchen," Maurice responded. When I got there, he was making my favorite breakfast.

"You must know you owe me," I teased. "You up in here making chicken and waffles like you always do when you get me into some shit I have no business doing."

"Bruh, you know I ain't know last night was gonna be Uber hell. Especially on a random weekday. Had I known—"

"You still would have asked me to take your shift," I interrupted.

He shrugged. "Yeah, I guess. Did anything happen worth mentioning? Seems like I'm always picking up folks near Santa Monica and Venice Beach. Folks be wildin' the later it gets."

My thoughts drifted to Burgundy and her adorable Sailor Moon pajamas. I'd actually told Mo about her months ago. Not her name, but the impression she'd left on me. Now that I knew she knew him too, I wanted to keep her real identity to myself.

"Nah, nothing worth mentioning."

He glanced my way as if he was trying to figure out if I was telling the truth or not. My cousin and I were close as hell, but he had a big ass mouth and was nosier than I was.

"Did you talk to your dad?" he asked, continuing with breakfast. "He called me several times."

"Nah, I sent him to voicemail," I told him, taking a swig of the cup of orange juice I'd just poured myself. "He calls me all the time about random shit. Since he's living in Florida now, I thought I'd get a break from receiving five calls a day."

Mo laughed. "Unc is just making up for lost time. He still feels guilty about not being in your life much growing up."

I didn't comment right away because I knew Mo was right. No doubt, my dad felt guilty. However, I'd witnessed firsthand how much my parents hated each other and even though I'd placed more blame on him throughout the years than my mom, it hadn't been fair. They were both at fault. Regardless, the devoted dad act was getting old.

"I'll call him back in a few."

"Good." Mo wrapped up breakfast and we both sat

down to eat, catching up like we hadn't been able to do in months since I'd been traveling a lot on different jobs. "Did you decide if you're going to keep renting that place you stayin' at down the street or finally going to buy you a place."

I shrugged. "I don't know man. Buying a place is so permanent. Plus, I'm gone most the time for work anyway."

"Only because you chose that life," Mo said. "You can take landscaping jobs in the state and not travel as much."

"For what?" I asked. "Besides you and your mom, I don't even have a lot of family here. My mom is always state hopping and my sisters both live out of state. Is there really a reason for me to be here when you and I can catch up any place?"

"When you put it that way, I guess not," he said.

What he wasn't saying was that he didn't understand how my job kept me so busy. But there was more to landscaping than mowing lawns and pulling weeds and luckily, I'd been blessed to work on some of the most beautiful yards on the west coast. Which brought my thoughts, once again, back to Burgundy and the reason I was back home in Inglewood.

But you missed your shot to tell her more, I told myself. When she'd mentioned her job and the fact that they'd let her go, it hadn't felt like the right time to tell her my news, although I had tried before she stopped me. She wouldn't have taken it well anyway. I knew Burgundy more than she thought I did. Granted, I had only officially met her a few months ago and hadn't expected to run into her while taking over Mo's Uber rides, but I shouldn't have been all that shocked.

My guys, and even Mo, used to tease me back in the day when I'd talk all that *destiny has other plans* stuff, but my gut hadn't steered me wrong yet. It seemed that no matter what had happened in my life lately, Burgundy was right there in the back of my mind. Her presence reminding me that if approached by the *right* woman, anything was possible.

CHAPTER 4

Iceland: Day Four
(five months ago)

Kane

I<small>T WAS</small> strange for me to have only known someone for four days, yet feel like I'd known them forever. That was what it felt like with Burgundy.

She was hesitant to get close to me that first day, but I hadn't been willing to ignore the connection I'd felt. It wasn't every day that I literally ran into a woman who I wanted to get to know on a more personal level.

My entire life I'd been a wanderer, so I didn't really have time to get into a serious relationship. According to my mom, she felt like I was always running from something. My sisters felt like I was always up to something. My dad never really seemed to have an opinion on me one way or the other. But my grandfather had never failed to sing a different tune because in Pops' eyes, I was always running toward something, I just had yet to find it.

"Where did you grow up?" I asked as we followed the tour group on a hike to Bruarfoss Waterfall, just outside of the small village of Laugarvatn. We were at the second location and even though the weather was still a little chilly, it wasn't nearly as cold as it had been at the mountain lodge we'd previously stayed at.

"I thought we agreed not to ask questions like that," she said.

I nodded. "We kinda said that. However, that was when we agreed not to look each other up on social media. I figured which state we were from was a safer topic."

What I didn't tell her was that I'd already had a suspicion we were from the same state. It was in the way she talked and the words she used. Her vernacular when her suitcase had finally been delivered to her. A couple places that she'd referenced or mumbled when she thought I wasn't paying attention.

She'd also gotten a couple calls while we'd been on a tour and although I hadn't been trying to overhear her conversations, I'd heard a few things that referenced places I was familiar with.

"Where do you think I'm from?" she asked.

"California," I said without hesitation. "Maybe LA or San Diego. And before you accuse me of looking you up, I was born and raised in Inglewood, so I know a Californian when I hear one."

She squinted her eyes, studying me to see if she

believed what I was saying. "How long have you known I'm from there?"

"I suspected it the first day," I told her honestly.

She nodded. "In that case, I gotta admit that before you even told me just now, I suspected you were from California too. The way you talked and certain words you used gave you away."

I laughed so loud, I got the attention of a couple others in our tour group. "Damn. And here I was thinking I was the only one who'd picked up on our similarities."

She snorted. "Similarities? I didn't say all that. All I meant was, I'd picked up on the fact that you may be from the west coast like me."

"Gotcha. So, which is it?" I asked.

"What do you mean?"

"Are you from LA or San Diego?"

"I'm from Crenshaw," she said with a big smile on her face.

I nodded. "So you're basically right down the street from me."

Her eyes widened. "Which doesn't matter because we won't reach out to each other past this trip."

"Your idea. Not mine."

She slapped me on the arm. "I'm serious. This trip is supposed to be about me doing some self-reflecting. I didn't count on you distracting me."

I smiled, not voicing how happy I was to be a distraction. Burgundy seemed to be one of those women who liked things to be a certain way and if anything happened outside of her bubble of comfort, she ran for the hills.

Conversation continued to flow between us as we

reached the waterfall, everyone around us taking out their cameras to capture the beauty around us. We'd been standing near the edge of the waterfall away from most of our group for a few minutes before I realized neither of us had taken out our phones to snap a pic. "Would you like me to take a photo of you?"

"Sure," she said, getting out her phone.

"I'll take it on mine," I told her after I observed both of our phones. When she looked at me questioningly, I explained that I had a more recent iPhone, so the camera was better.

In all honesty, that was only partially true. I did have a better camera on my phone, but I also wanted to have a pic to remember this trip just in case I didn't get an opportunity to take another one of her.

She stood in the typical one hand on hip with head tilted to the side pose that I captured right away. I took a few more shots as she changed poses noting that she had some of the most striking features I'd ever seen in a woman.

Although she was dressed for the chilly weather, I didn't forget how sexy her curvy body looked underneath her coat. She'd been wearing one of those sweater dresses yesterday morning at breakfast and while most of the people at our table were discussing how great the eggs and croissants were, I was observing Burgundy, noting that she'd curled her black bob and put on some red gloss that lightly smeared every time she ate.

She was a vision and every time she walked into a room, so poised, yet sexy, every tourist in our group took notice. Her deep, chestnut brown eyes were vibrant and every day, I noticed she seemed to get more and more comfortable with me.

"Up for a selfie?" I asked. She nodded without hesitation, which surprised me because Burgundy had been giving me a hard time about even the small things. However, for a guy like me, it was part of her charm. I wouldn't say I was always up for a chase, but I was guilty of getting bored easily and Burgundy had been keeping me on my toes with her sassy mouth.

And to think, I'd dreaded the weather the entire flight to Iceland only to stumble into a beautiful brown beauty who was making this trip ten times better than I ever could have imagined.

"Check out that path," I mentioned, after we'd finished taking pictures. Her eyes followed my line of vision.

"Looks like no one is headed that way," she said.

I nodded my head in the direction of the path. "Let's go."

Her eyes widened. "Oh nah, I'm not going down a sketchy path in a country that I don't know that well. That's how people end up missing."

"It's probably safe. It's just, everyone in our tour group is staying together, but there is plenty for us to explore."

"Not me. I'm more of a look-but-don't-explore kind of girl."

"I thought this trip was about taking chances," I teased. "Some of the best experiences happen off the beaten path. Plus, I'm here with you. You don't have to worry."

She squinted at me and seemed to be weighing her options. "Okay, let's go. But if we run into something we have no business messing with, I am hightailing my ass right back to the tour group."

I was still laughing as we started the journey down the path. Just as I'd suspected, it was breathtaking with green plants mixed in with snow, the scenery making little sense to me, but looking beautiful nonetheless.

"Wow, good choice," she said, walking a little ahead of me. So much about Burgundy was surprising and I wondered if she even knew what impact she was having on me in just a few short days.

"Do you travel a lot?" I asked her.

"Not really," she said. "I'm so involved with work that I don't really have much time, but when I do travel, it's always for at least seven days. You mentioned that you travel a lot, so what has been your favorite country so far?"

"Iceland," I stated, without hesitation.

She glanced over her shoulder and rolled her eyes at me. "I'm being serious, what's your favorite country?"

"I'm being serious too," I confirmed. "There are so many hidden treasures in this country and I've never been to a place that can be warm in one location and freezing a few feet away. Plus, all the lagoons and water-falls are some of the best I've seen."

She sighed. "This place really is amazing. I hadn't been sure I was going to like Iceland as much as I do, but this place is surprisingly relaxing."

"And meeting me has been pretty damn great too, huh?"

Her laugh was so infectious, I immediately began laughing along with her. "I guess meeting you has been okay," she said.

"Just okay?"

"Yeah, just okay."

I caught up to her and fell into step beside her.

"Well, meeting you on this trip has been the highlight of my year."

She rolled her eyes again. "Always the charmer."

"Only when I'm trying to charm you." That earned me another giggle, but I really wasn't playing. Burgundy was worth any effort and truth was, she was already having an impact on me.

"You're too much," she said, shaking her head. "Does this usually work on other women?"

I shrugged. "Honestly, I don't even flirt that much, let alone date. Somewhere along the line, I decided to invest myself mostly in my work and kinda pushed everything else aside."

"Hmm." She glanced at me before looking back ahead of her.

"And what does *hmm* mean?"

"Nothing much," she explained. "It's just, I'm the same way when it comes to my job. A workaholic with no time for much else."

"Except traveling." I waved my arms around us. "Workaholic or not, this trip is for pleasure, am I right?"

"It depends on your definition of pleasure."

"You better be careful when you make a statement like that," I warned. "You may get an answer you're not ready for."

She slowly stopped her stride and faced me. "There's not much that surprises me, Kane. Or in your case, I know the kind of person you are, so that means, I'm less surprised."

"Oh yeah?" I stepped closer to her, the fog of my breath hitting the cold air mingling between us. "After four days, you already have me pegged, huh? So tell me, what is it that you think you know about me?"

Instead of stepping back, she held her head high, her eyes filled with determination to prove me wrong. "You're the type of guy who acts all nice and innocent, but he always has a hidden agenda. Don't get me wrong, you do nice shit, but you also make calculated moves."

"Moves like what?" I challenged, enjoying this side of her.

"Like, how at breakfast this morning, we were all supposed to rotate seats to get to know others in the tour group, yet, you convinced the guide that I was nervous about being in a foreign country and needed your support. So we remained seated next to one another."

I didn't deny what she'd claimed, but I was a bit surprised she knew how I'd convinced one of the tour guides to let us sit together this morning. My best guess was the guide had mentioned something to her.

"And on that first day we met, you somehow convinced the hotel receptionist to put us on the same floor."

"No I didn't," I lied.

"Yes, you did. You were originally two floors above me, but the next morning, I found out you'd switched floors. My guess is that you told them you had an issue with the water pressure in your room's shower or something."

I nodded my head, impressed by her observation. She was partially right. I'd done some of my best convincing to get the hotel staff to put me on her floor, claiming I often got anxiety being on higher floors. It was a shitty lie, but it had worked.

"But that wasn't the most strategic thing you've done since we've met." She closed the last couple inches between us, my eyes suddenly fixated on her long eyelashes. "You're most calculated move thus far was the way you convinced me to get closer to this path for pictures, when actually, you just wanted to get me alone."

My eyes held hers, the moment between us electric even in the cold. Up until now, we'd kept things pretty PG. Yet, I couldn't deny that I'd thought about kissing her ever second since I'd run into her in the airport.

And she knew it too. I could tell in the way she lightly rubbed her lips together and studied my eyes. The weather was no joke, but I didn't even feel cold being this close to her, the heat radiating from our bodies overtaking my mind when I asked, "And knowing this, you still decided to walk with me? So maybe this instant connection I feel isn't so one sided?"

"It's not." She answered quicker than I'd expected. "In fact, the realist in me is having major issues with how strong our attraction is to one another."

She wasn't lying. Temptation was slapping me across the damn face where she was concerned. Yet, I could see the apprehension in her eyes and felt a need to remind her that, "Sometimes, the most unexpected connection could be just what you need at the exact time you need it. The key is not to overthink it, but accept it for what it is."

She giggled, her eyes boldly dropping to my lips. "Why do you always sound like you're quoting some philosophy book?"

"Fun fact," I told her, inching my head to hers. "I was never that great in philosophy." I watched her slow intake of breath as I got closer, mesmerized by the fact that she had me so hooked after such a short period of time.

"I find that hard to believe," she whispered, slightly leaning on her tiptoes.

"Believe me, I didn't understand it much." Our mouths grew even closer, the slowness of the moment already proving that a kiss that hadn't even happened yet was destined to be one of those moments one could rarely repeat in life.

"Now, if we're talking about chemistry," I muttered. "I aced that shit."

Not waiting any longer, I gently placed my lips on hers, our greedy mouths connecting in a way that didn't surprise me at all.

I knew kissing Burgundy would be good as shit. I knew her plush lips were even softer than they looked. I knew hugging her curvy body would give me all kinds of dirty thoughts since I couldn't seem to be around this woman for longer than a few seconds and not think about doing naughty things to her.

We weren't halfway done with the trip yet, but I was already regretting that my time with her would be cut short. Yeah, we may have lived in the same state, but getting a woman like Burgundy to give a guy like me a chance to pursue her was going to take much more than wishful thinking.

CHAPTER 5

Burgundy

"*A*re you sure you don't want to just bring me to work and take the car?"

"I'm good with the bus, Aunt Rach. I'm only going to Park Manor because Teegan begged me to come and tell her what happened."

Aunt Rach looked at me questioningly, but didn't say more. However, I knew deep down she was curious why I didn't just tell Teegan to come to her place rather than go to the place that had just let me go.

Truth was, since it had happened a week ago, I'd already heard from a lot of residents who knew what had happened and folks were saying that they understood why I would never come back to Park Manor. Everyone seemed to hate how I was treated, but I didn't want them to think that Larry and the good ol' boys club had gotten to me.

"I could still ring his neck," Aunt Rach said, refer-ring to Larry. "After everything you've done for that job, they let you go because of a stupid degree. Do they have no loyalty?"

"They don't know the definition of the word," I told her. "It's not like it was back in the day. Companies today feel like they don't owe you anything."

"Such a shame." She shook her head while gath-ering her purse and work bag to head out. She was a nurse at one of the best hospitals in LA and although she'd told me she could get me a job at the hospital, I passed. I'd worked there for a short stint before working at Park Manor and hadn't cared for it.

After I said bye to my aunt, I made my way to the bus stop and was glad that I only had to wait a couple minutes before it arrived. It had been years since I'd taken the bus and I had to admit, I hadn't missed it.

I wasn't one of those types of women who felt like they were too good for the bus, but I wasn't a fan of public transportation in general. *Real rich for someone without a car,* I thought to myself.

When I reached Park Manor, it took all of my energy to hold my head high as I greeted Norman and walked past a couple residents who shot me looks of pity or told me they were sorry I'd lost my job. I reached Teegan's door in record time and before I could even knock, she answered.

"B, I am so sorry," she yelped, pulling me into her condo. "I hope you know that we filed a complaint with management about this and am hoping they realize they can't function without you."

"Who's we?" I asked, dropping my purse on a chair I passed on our way to her living room. My question was answered the moment I saw three other sets of eyes looking my way.

"Ah." I looked from Sky, Paityn, and Kathi to a sheepish Teegan. "Tee, I had no idea I was meeting with all the ladies."

"It's not her fault," Sky said. "We figured she knew what had happened and when she mentioned that she'd see you today, we begged her to tell us what time."

I snorted, appreciating their gesture, but knowing that they hadn't begged Teegan for anything. Something told me my girl had been too pissed not to spill the beans.

"Well, I appreciate you all for caring," I told the group, hugging each of them before taking a seat on the couch. "Honestly, I wanted to see you ladies the moment I got the news. I guess I'm still a little shocked that I'm out of a job right now."

"It's bullshit," Paityn said. "To let you go over something so small is crazy."

"Some folks don't see not having a degree as something small," Kathi stated before turning to me with wide eyes. "But personally, I don't think it's a big deal at all. I just meant that some jobs care about that stuff."

"You're right," I said. "I guess I get why it would be an issue, but I thought I'd proved myself at the job enough to have it not be a factor."

"You have," Teegan retorted. "Don't doubt that you are the best leasing manager Park Manor ever had."

"Not to mention, you were the tenant-proclaimed special events director as well," Paityn added. "Always planning things for residents and renters to bring everyone closer together. No one else in your office did that."

I sighed. "I know you're right, but I just hate that everyone is looking at me as if I'm uneducated and was never a person worthy of having a job at a place like this."

Kathi, who was seated the closest to me, placed a hand on my forearm. "They're just judgmental and can't see past their own insecurities. You're great at your job and Park Manor needs you."

"I need Park Manor more," I mumbled under my breath. I had no idea how what I would do next, now that I was out of a job. And I still had bills to pay too. I wasn't looking forward to filing for unemployment, but I needed that check so I'd have to check my pride at the door.

"That's enough about me," I announced once I felt myself getting all in my feelings again. "What's new with you all?"

Teegan gave me a look like she wanted to still talk about me and my unfortunate circumstances, but luckily, Sky changed the subject.

"Did you gals see that new mural that was painted in West Hollywood for Nipsey Hussle?"

I nodded my head. "It's beautiful, right? So many artistic works in his honor are popping up around the city, but I think that's one of my favs."

"Mine too!" Sky exclaimed, diving into some other things she'd spotted as a new California resident.

We were deep in conversation going from topic to topic like we usually did when we were together, when a text message came through. I rolled my eyes as I glanced at my phone. "Ugh. It's Larry."

Paityn pretended to gag. "What does he want?"

"It doesn't say, but he heard I was in the building and asked me to come down to the office."

"You don't have to go," Teegan said. "But if you do and he says something about you not coming to Park Manor anymore, I'll sic the hounds on him."

"You have a dog?" Sky asked.

Teegan shook her head. "No, but I've lived in this building for so long that I know exactly who to loop in if we need reinforcements." Her eyes widened. "Or maybe we could even strike."

"What would we strike?" Kathi asked.

"Not paying mortgage or rent until Burgundy gets her job back."

All of the ladies pinned her with a look of disbelief, myself included. "Uh, maybe we'll save the Park Manor strike for another issue," I suggested. "No point in having more folks evicted."

Teegan shrugged. "I guess."

I was still laughing at Teegan's look of disappointment after I'd said my goodbyes and headed to meet Larry. I loved that my girls would put their heart and soul into a cause, but I wasn't trying to have people at odds over me.

It was almost an out-of-body experience walking back into the office after everything that had happened last time I was there. I'd expected more people to be around and was surprised when the phone rang several times with no answer. Larry was big on answering the phone before it reached the fourth ring.

"Hello? Is anyone here?" Since he'd texted me, I assumed at least Larry was here. When the phone rang again, I decided to answer it out of habit. It was one of the older Park Manor residents and although I was sure she'd heard I was let go, she filed her complaint about the renter next door to her as if she didn't care that I technically didn't work at Park Manor anymore.

Doing what I did best, I got all the details and ensured her that I would tell Larry about her situation so that he could handle it promptly. It wasn't until I disconnected the call that I realized Larry had returned.

"Burgundy, I'm so happy to see you," he said, motioning for me to join him in his office. Reluctantly, I followed, confused as to why he seemed excited to see me. "Thank you for responding to my message."

"You're welcome," I said, taking a seat. "But I am surprised that you said you're happy to see me after practically kicking me out without even giving me time to say my goodbyes."

"That was a mistake on my part," Larry said. "Please accept this as my formal apology. I never should have dismissed you the way I did. You've contributed quite a bit to the Park Manor leasing team and it hasn't been the same without you."

I raised an eyebrow. "Is this your way of giving me my job back?"

"No," he said with an unnecessary quickness. "But I did ask you here to offer you another job with Park Manor instead."

Crossing my arms over my chest, I studied his face to see if he was serious. "I'm listening."

Larry cleared his throat four times and cracked his neck in that annoying way that he did whenever he was putting off talking about something he didn't want to talk about. Either that, or he was nervous about how the other party would take his words.

"Here's the thing, Burgundy. We need you around

here, but you don't meet the requirements for a leasing agent, so we can't have you working for a prestigious establishment like Park Manor in a high-level position."

"This job isn't rocket science, Larry," I deadpanned. "I'm excellent at what I do and my retention numbers have been the highest on the team since I started working here. Nick and Colin may have masters degrees, but they have never met their quota since being employed here."

He waved a finger in the air. "Yes, but they also didn't lie on their applications."

You've gotta be shittin' me. I doubted Colin had ever really worked for President Obama's campaign like he claimed, which was a big reason why he got the job because he'd tanked his hands-on training. Yet, instead of throwing Colin under the bus, I asked Larry, "Why does it seem like you put an effort forth to investigate my background after years of me making you look good as the Property Manager, but failed to do so with your other employees?"

He frowned and leaned back in his desk chair. "See, Burgundy. Your mouth may be the reason you don't get the job that I'm offering you with Park Manor."

It took all of my energy not to roll my eyes. "What's the job, Larry?"

"Well, as you know since we lost Candy, we've gone through several temps for the office assistant role."

"You can't be serious," I stated. "You want me to go from a leasing manager to an office assistant?"

"Not just your regular run of the mill assistant. You'll also be in charge of a few special events we have lined up through the rest of the year."

"Events that I set up prior to you letting me go," I added.

"Uh, right," he confirmed. "But the best part is, you'll only be taking a twenty-five thousand dollar pay cut."

Ha! Only as if that's not a lot. "So basically, I'd be making the same amount Candy did when she worked here."

He nodded. "Exactly. Do we have a deal?"

"No, we don't." I stood up and walked out his office, pissed that I'd even given him a minute of my time.

"Burgundy, maybe you should think about the offer," he said, lagging behind me. I was actually shocked that his lazy ass had gotten out of his desk chair to follow me. "We need you. Please at least think about it."

"I have thought about it, Larry. And the answer is a firm no."

"Okay, what if I increase your pay by five thousand dollars?"

I shook my head as I reached the front door. "Nope. Not good enough."

"Ten thousand," he retorted.

"Negative."

He groaned. "Fifteen thousand."

There was something about the desperation in his voice that made me stop in my tracks. I'd known Larry for a while and if he was begging me to come back, then shit must really be bad. "I'll tell you what. I'll come back as the office assistant if you agree to pay me the base salary I was making as a leasing manager."

His eyes grew wide. "That's blasphemy and unheard of for an office assistant."

"It may be a little high, but you and I both know I

wasn't getting paid what I was worth anyway." I gave him a look that dared him to challenge me. "Besides, I used to make commission and I lose that being an assistant, so that's my counter. Plus, I at least want the title of leasing specialist instead of office assistant. And given what I'll have to do to rectify the damage I'm sure you all have done in the week I was gone, I'm sure you'll agree that it's better suited. Take it or leave it, Larry."

He ran his sweaty hands down his face, shaking his head in a way that forced me to focus on his bald spot. "Okay," he snarled. "No pay cut. New title. I'll email you the contract within the hour, but if I abide by your terms, you start tomorrow."

"That won't work," I told him. "Your last contract screwed me over, so I'll be having my lawyer look at this one. She'll need at least a day or two, so I'll start after it's reviewed and adjusted to my liking."

He looked as if he wanted to spit fire in my direction as he let out a terse, "Fine."

It took all of my energy not to jump up and down as I exited the office. I really loved Park Manor and even though the property office was filled with a bunch of entitled assholes, I knew I was a small reason residents and tenants were so happy. Taking out my phone, I shot a quick text to Skylar, Paityn, Teegan, and Kathi telling them that I'd be working at Park Manor again. I was just rounding the corner towards the lobby when I ran into a wall of pure, solid muscle.

"Shit," I yelped, trying to catch my phone as it slipped from my fingers. In my mind, I was already mentally preparing for it to fall and crack on the stone floor, but surprisingly, my roadblock caught it.

"Thanks," I whispered as I accepted my phone. "What are you doing at Park Manor?"

"Wow. No hi first?" Kane teased.

"My bad." I cleared my throat. "Hey Kane, fancy seeing you here."

He laughed. "Hi Burgundy, I didn't expect to see you here either, but glad I ran into you." His eyes briefly went up and down the length of my body. He was smooth with it, but I'd caught him anyway.

"What are you doing here?" I asked again. "Visiting a girlfriend?"

He shook his head. "Nah. I don't have a girlfriend. I was contracted to update the landscape, including a new outdoor terrace and garden."

"That's right," I said. "I almost forgot that they were expanding the rooftop space. But I wasn't aware that they'd hired anyone for that project."

He smiled, my eyes going straight to his lips like they always did. "They hired yours truly. And I meant to tell you that when I dropped you off at your aunt's a week ago but got sidetracked."

"No worries." I vaguely recalled him getting ready to tell me something and me cutting him off, but honestly, I didn't even mind that he hadn't said anything. "Congrats on landing the contract. I heard quite a few landscape artists bid on it."

"Thanks. I only started on everything a couple days ago, so it's a long way to go before I'm finished. Were you visiting some friends?"

"At first I was, but my manager and I sorted some things out and I'll be working here again," I explained.

"That's great. Will you be living here again too?"

"Living here?" It wasn't until Kane had voiced those

words that I realized I hadn't even demanded that Larry let me move back into my apartment as well. A part of me was annoyed that I'd forgotten such a big factor, yet, the other part of me thought that maybe it was a sign that living at the same place I worked wasn't that healthy. "No, I won't be living here. I'll probably stay with my aunt until I find another place to live."

He nodded. "Then I guess now is my chance to ask you to go on a date with me tonight."

I laughed. "Real smooth, Kane."

"You already know how smooth I can be," he said, his eyes catching mine. "I'm also straightforward and you never contacted me, so if you still won't give me your number, meet me here in the lobby at eight o'clock." With that said, he placed a soft kiss on the back of my hand and began walking to the elevators.

"How do you know I don't already have a date tonight?" I yelled.

"I don't," he said. "I'm just hoping if another guy asked you out, you'd show up here tonight instead because you'd rather be with me."

He hopped on the elevator and waved just before the door closed, leaving me to think about his offer. The old Burgundy would have pretended like she didn't want to date him, but there was no point pretending. Even so, I was nervous for reasons I didn't understand.

CHAPTER 6

I̶celand: Day Nine…
(five months ago)

Burgundy

"This has been my favorite stop so far," I told Kane as we sat in the lavish living room chairs of our suite that overlooked our own private lagoon. The last stop on our tour was a luxurious stay at a gorgeous hotel overlooking Blue Lagoon, that was known as one of the twenty-five wonders of the world.

The entire day had been magical and the geothermal seawater of the lagoon was one of the most relaxing experiences I'd ever had. The fact that I'd been able to share the experience with Kane had been icing on the cake.

"Are you freaked out that we're sharing a suite yet?" he asked.

Both of us were still wrapped in the plush white robes the resort had provided us with and until now, we hadn't discussed the room situation.

When we'd arrived this morning, our tour guide had informed us that anyone who wanted to upgrade their stay would be able to get a private lagoon suite since surprisingly, they'd had a couple left due to cancellations. Kane and I had both wanted the experience and since it was so expensive and only two for excited parties in our tour group to snag, we acted quickly and sharing a suite had just made sense.

However, if Kane was picking up on the fact that I hadn't shared a room with a man overnight in a while, he'd be correct in that assessment. Still, I couldn't let him know he made me nervous. "I'm good. We're both adults and sharing a room doesn't mean anything will happen that I don't want to happen."

He took a sip of the cognac he'd ordered. "And what do you want to happen tonight?"

"Ah." *Shit.* What did I want to happen? Granted, we'd been spending a lot of time together and I was well aware that it was the last night of our tour before we had to head home. And of course, I'd thought about sleeping with almost every day of this trip. But I wasn't the type to have a fling on a vacation. I was more the type to overanalyze the situation the entire time and head back home wondering *what if.*

"Maybe I should rephrase my question," he said when I didn't respond right away. Grabbing my chair and turning it away from the window, he pulled me closer to him. "If I kissed you right now, would you stop me?"

I shook my head. "No."

He leaned closer, his lips hovering over mine. "If I don't stop at just your mouth, will you let me continue kissing other parts of your body?"

I nodded my head, unable to do anything but agree. "Yes." I wasn't sure what was happening between us in that moment, but I didn't want to break the spell he had over me. The eyes that had brought me comfort throughout the trip were now making me ache, causing me to clinch my legs together. His mouth that had been making me laugh during every bus ride was now making my breath catch as he placed soft kisses along my collarbone.

Normally, I was the type of woman who'd act like she hadn't expected for the night to take us in this direction, but like I kept reminding myself, the new and improved Burgundy didn't play games. I'd known damn well what I was doing when I agreed to share a suite with Kane and now, he was proving that splurging on an expensive ass suite in a magical one-of-a-kind place wouldn't go to waste.

"No matter what happens," he said. "I've enjoyed our time together."

"You've been okay," I said with a shrug. "I guess you're better company than my guys Jim, Jack, John, and Jamie."

He went to talk, but coughed before he got his words out. "Hold up. You got four other dudes?"

I looked his way as I took another sip of my wine, taking my sweet time to answer. "I love hanging out with my men," I finally said. "But never at the same time… unless I'm feeling frisky." His eyes widened and he looked downright shocked.

"One of my friends once told me that she'd never seen me more faithful to four men in my life," I continued. "When I'm feeling playful, I tell John I need a good time. Yet, when Jim calls out my name, I'm all his for the night." I played with the rim of my wine glass, watching Kane through lowered eyelids. "Jamie is always down for a good fuck and a woman needs to be able to count on a man to give her the rough shit."

Leaning closer to him, I whispered, "But none of my guys can work me like Jack can." I was close enough to place a kiss on Kane's neck, grateful he didn't stop me. "He knows my weaknesses. He knows my secrets. He can touch me in ways the others can't. One sip of his deliciousness and I'm done."

I was looking into his eyes when understanding hit. "You're talking about whiskey," he stated. "At least, I hope like hell you're talking about liquor 'cause I'm way too turned on by this shit for you to be talking about some other dudes."

I kissed his neck again. "If you mean Jim Bean, Jack Daniels, Johnnie Walker and Jameson, then yeah, my dark and delicious guys are whiskey."

"I'm getting you back for that," he warned.

"If you must, I have an idea," I whispered, my mouth hovering over his ear. "I want you to fuck me."

He leaned up to look at my face and smirked. "I knew you had a naughty mouth. Tryin' to act like nothing I've been doing this whole trip has been affecting you like you've been affecting me."

"Gotta keep you wanting more," I told him, before

taking his face into my hands and kissing him with more passion than I had the entire trip. This kiss was nothing like our stolen pecks and was even more heightened than the first kiss we'd shared.

He pulled me from my chair, his arms wrapping around me as he quickly took control of the kiss. Our mouths melted together in a way that said we knew tonight was our last night together. The night where we allowed our bodies to say the words that we'd never release from our mouths.

Even though we were from California, we'd agreed not to look each other up after this trip. Our conversations had been some of the best I'd ever had, but we'd managed not to say too much about our private lives, while saying a lot at the same time.

We fell into the bed with a fluidity that I didn't expect since it felt like tonight was a long time coming. Or at least, it felt as long as it could have, given that we'd only known each other for nine days. Yet, they were nine days I didn't think I could ever forget. Nine days of me getting to know a stranger and genuinely being invested in what he was saying. Nine days of a man learning things about me that some close to me didn't know.

Nine days of him sharing details about his strained relationship with his father while I confided in him about my mother's alcoholism that eventually led to her death. The stories we'd shared while touring the most intriguing country I'd ever visited were those that didn't seem fit for a conversation between strangers. Which made me question if that's all we were to each other? Strangers who'd kept each other company during the cold Icelandic nights of a ten-day tour or a man and woman brought together by a stronger force that I didn't believe in. Fate as some would call it.

He untied my robe and made quick work of my bikini, while my hands got to work on his robe as I pulled down his trunks and discarded them with the rest of our clothes. Our kissing grew more frantic when our naked bodies caressed one another, every nerve standing to full attention at the heat we were generating.

Kane briefly stopped our lip lock, his eyes pinning me in a way that let me know he was waiting for confirmation to continue. And while my verbal okay was probably what he preferred, I gave him a head nod, unable to trust my mouth to voice my okay when the only sounds being released from my lips were moans of satisfaction.

I wasn't even sure where the condom had come from, but he slid it on with ease and dropped his lips back to mine at the same time that he slid inside me in one fluid stroke. I cried out in pleasure at the way he felt inside me and when he began to move in his own powerful rhythm, it was pure perfection.

"I'm going to lift you, okay?"

I nodded right before he sat me up, his dick never leaving my core. I'd never had sex in a seated position and a part of me worried that I might feel too heavy in his lap. However, that notion was quickly thrown out the window as he pounded into me, while lifting me at the same time as if my weight wasn't shit compared to what he lifted in the gym.

Oh, fuck. He was hitting spots that I swore had never been touched before and it made me wonder how I'd ever not try and find him in California when I knew what homeboy was packing underneath his jeans.

In fact, a part of me was worried that I never should have dove into this in the first place. That sex with Kane was always bound to be complicated because I liked him a little too much and our connection was way too strong.

Stop thinking, I warned myself. *Just feel*. It didn't do either of us any good pretending we were more than we were and that this wasn't just a one night stand between two strangers who'd met on vacation. Any thoughts that had been floating around in my mind ceased the moment I felt myself reach the point of no return, my orgasm creeping up on me quick. I wanted to warn him and let him know I was close. But it hit like a hurricane, my insides clenching around him, causing him to follow closely behind me.

I held him as he rode out the last of his pleasure and kissed his shoulders with the same tenderness that he'd kissed my collarbone earlier. When we finally felt semi normal, he pulled my face to his for a passionate kiss that I felt all the way to my toes.

Throughout the entire trip, Kane and I hadn't been able to keep quiet and had talked to one another more than I was sure either of us had ever planned on talking to another person during our solo trips. Ironic that my solo trip felt more like a romantic excursion than anything.

"I'm not sure I'll get enough of you," Kane whispered, catching me off guard. *Enough of me?* It didn't seem like the right time to remind him that tomorrow was the last day of our trip. That tonight was our last time together, leaving only stolen moments that we'd have to capture in the morning.

So, instead of breaking the lustful fog we found

ourselves in, I admitted, "I'm not sure I'll get enough of you either." And damn did I mean that shit.

* * *

Kane

SHE WAS DIFFERENT THIS MORNING. More relaxed. Stress-free. I'd only known her a short while, but I couldn't recall a time during the entire trip where I'd seen her look more content than I did now and deep down, I knew I had something to do with that.

Last night had been amazing and while I hadn't wanted the night to end, I wasn't too sure I could have gone a fourth round of sex with Burgundy. She was the type of woman a man got addicted to and I refused to admit that I was already hooked.

"Are you going to eat your breakfast or stare at me until we have to pack up and check out?" she asked.

"Let's not let this be the end," I blurted. "We both live near LA. Let's continue what we've started here in Iceland."

I'd been going back and forth all morning on whether I should be honest or keep my feelings to myself. Judging by the look of panic on her face, I'd made the wrong call. I could already see her second-guessing what we'd done.

"I knew we shouldn't have had sex," she said. "I told you at the beginning of the tour that this trip was supposed to be me figuring some shit out. You were a distraction I never saw coming and yeah, we had a good time together, but last night was a one-time thing."

More like a three-time thing, but I wasn't about to correct her right now. "You don't feel like maybe we were supposed to meet on this trip? Like maybe it was fate telling us that there is more to life than work?"

"I don't believe in fate," she said. "Fate wouldn't have taken my mom from me when I was younger and I told you, the day she died was the day I stopped believing in fate."

I reached across the table and grabbed her hand. "I understand why you feel that way, but can you admit that we have something worth exploring? We met for a reason."

"Or maybe we met for just one night," she said, removing her hand from mine. When she stood from her chair and pulled her t-shirt over her thick thighs that I'd been admiring all morning, I felt a shift take place in the room as I watched her stare out at the scenery.

"I didn't mean to make you uncomfortable," I told her. "And I didn't mean to mess up our good morning either." I stood and walked toward her, placing a soft kiss on her shoulder when I reached her. "We still have two hours before we have to be out of here and back with the tour group. So how about you forget what I suggested earlier and instead, we make these last moments count."

My heart was beating a mile a minute when I whispered those words to her. It was crazy to think that ten days ago, we were strangers. Yet now, I was hanging onto the moment with all that I could, knowing that making the most of the time we had left was all she would promise me today.

When she finally said, "Yes, let's make these last moments count," I didn't waste any time turning her to face me and capturing her lips the way I had several times throughout this trip. I wanted her to remember me. I wanted her to remember us. And if luck was on my side, this wouldn't be the last time we'd see each other.

CHAPTER 7

Kane

There were times when I'd tell myself not to get my hopes up because even though I was a glass half full type of guy, things happened. Shit that you couldn't control no matter how badly you wanted the circumstances to be different.

Yet, over the years I'd learned to read people and situations in a way that helped me keep my expectations in check. Meaning, if I asked someone a certain question, I was prepared for how I thought they may answer. Or if I was approached by something that I didn't want to do, I took into account the person and how they'd react to soften the blow. For some reason, all of that type of thinking went out the window when Burgundy Anderson was involved. I could have sworn when I mentioned a date tonight, she'd given me mad vibes that she'd be down for it too.

i

Walking up the stairs to her aunt's house, I refused to question if what I was doing made sense or not. I only knocked once before someone opened the door. A beautiful woman who seemed more like she could be her sister than her aunt.

"Can I help you?" she asked.

I stuck out my hand to greet her. "Hi, my name is Kane Brooks and I was hoping that Burgundy may be home. I'm a friend of hers from Park Manor."

The woman smiled in amusement before taking my hand. "I'm her aunt and I must say when my niece told me she'd run into a man at Park Manor who wouldn't take no for an answer, I'd assumed you were some overweight older gentlemen with a bad toupee and the notion that pursuing my niece wasn't cheating on his wife."

Well damn. "Uh, I can assure you ma'am, I'm none of the above. And your niece never gave me a direct no for our date tonight."

"But she never said yes either, am I right?" she asked.

"No ma'am, she didn't." I let out a sigh. "I just wanted to catch up with her. Is she home?"

"No, she isn't."

I nodded. "Okay. I'm sorry to have wasted your time, but I hope you enjoy the rest of your night."

"You too," she said, squinting her eyes. "I shouldn't tell you this because my niece would kill me, but she's attending one of those art experiences downtown tonight. I believe she was going solo, but I don't know the exact address since she took an Uber."

I nodded. "I see. It sounds like fun."

"She knew the driver who picked her up. Called him Mo. And from what she's told me, you're his cousin."

"She's told you about me?" I couldn't even hide the surprise in my voice.

"Yes, she did," her aunt said. "And if you want my advice, a woman like Burgundy will only give you a hard time if you're worth the effort. My niece is a no-nonsense kind of girl and from what I saw, you handled her really well when you dropped her off last week."

"Uh, I thought you weren't home when we'd arrived."

She pointed to her doorbell. "I have the Ring device, so I saw the entire thing. When you arrived tonight, I recalled your face from the day you dropped her off. You looked better on my Ring device than you did on the picture she showed me of you on her phone."

I laughed. "Thanks, I think." I remembered the moment she'd snapped the picture at the end of our vacation. I'd had pics that I had taken of her on my phone that I'd meant to airdrop her before we parted ways, yet, somehow it had slipped both of our minds.

"She told me a lot about you," I told her. "So, I'm glad I got a chance to meet you in person."

She smiled. "If you play your cards right, this won't be the last time we see one another, young man."

Aunt Rach and I exchanged a few more words before I left to go find my girl. I waited until I got in my car to call Mo.

"I was wondering when yo' ass would call me about Burgundy," he said without even greeting me.

"You know about us?" I asked. I knew Mo and he usually wasn't a good listener because he rarely picked up on certain shit.

"Did I know you were feelin' Burgundy before tonight? Nah. But she was asking me questions about you when I picked her up though and I got it out of her. She said you'd helped her after she'd gotten let go."

"And she's the one from Iceland," I added, coming clean. "The one I'd told you about months ago when I got back from my trip."

"Yo, she's the one who had you acting like Iceland had given you the key to the whole damn world."

I laughed. "I don't know about all that, but she was the main reason I enjoyed the trip as much as I did. We'd agreed not to see each other, but then, you asked me to take over your Uber rides that day and as luck would have it, Burgundy was my last ride."

"So what you're sayin' is that you gave me so much shit for helping me out, when I'm the reason you found the woman you haven't stopped telling me about since Iceland?"

I frowned. "Man, let's not act like we're even for all the times you've asked me to do some shit for you."

"Bruh, talkin' like that, you'd think you didn't want to know where I dropped your girl off at. Alone. By herself since she mentioned going solo to an event."

"Where did you drop her off at?" I asked.

"I can't tell you man," he said. "It's against protocol."

"You weren't talkin' all that protocol mess when you asked me to take over your Uber rides. If someone had known I wasn't you, but was driving your SUV and pretending to be, that shit could've meant your job."

He grew quiet, supposedly thinking about what I'd said. "Man, let me stop playing with you. I'll text you the address, but if Burgundy gets on all that confidently bullshit, don't tell her you got the address from me."

I didn't even bother responding to his request. Of course I was telling Burgundy that Mo had given me her location. I wasn't trying to be out here looking like a stalker.

* * *

Burgundy

"You're welcome." I read Aunt Rach's message aloud for the third time as I waited for her to respond to my question asking what she was talking about. My aunt was a straight shooter and rarely spoke in code, so I didn't understand why she wasn't messaging me right back explaining.

I was even more confused when her next text said, "You'll see." I groaned. "What will I see Aunt Rach," I whisper-yelled to my phone. I wasn't trying to sound crazy around all the strangers standing in line to get into the art experience, but she had me baffled.

Luckily, the line moved pretty fast and when the first large art room that attendees were able to view came into sight, I quickly dropped my quest to decipher the text messages. Little did I know they'd all make sense the moment I was approached by, "Kane?"

He shuffled around a few people until he reached me. "Do you have any idea long I've been looking for you?"

"I just got in," I told him. "How long have you been here?"

"Long enough. I've already been in several rooms and from the looks of it, there are plenty more."

"Yeah, it's a twenty-nine room exhibit, each room designed by a different local artist. Since it's November, the rooms are themed around the holidays. I've been trying to get here for weeks, but tickets were always sold out."

"That explains why it cost me two hundred dollars to pay a guy standing in line for his ticket," he said.

My eyes widened. "You paid someone that much for a ticket? What for?"

"I knew you'd be here," he said matter-of-factly.

"How did you know that?"

"I met your aunt," he explained.

"You're joking right? You went to my aunt's house?"

"Yeah, I did. She seems like a great woman and for a minute, I didn't know if she was actually your aunt or a sibling."

"Black don't crack," I stated with a laugh. "Now that I'm older, a lot of people confuse us for sisters."

"I'm not surprised," he said. "Why didn't you just tell me about your plans earlier?"

"You didn't really give me a chance," I explained.

"You have my number. You could have texted me."

He was right. I did have his number, and he still didn't have mine. "Truthfully? I think there was a part of me that wanted you to track me down."

He shook his head. "So you assumed I'd go see your aunt?"

"Not exactly. Did Mo tell you that I asked him to

pick me up and just paid him on the side what it would cost if I'd requested an Uber?"

Kane laughed. "Hell nah, that dude didn't tell me that shit."

"Well, I figured he'd mention something to you."

"He is the reason I know where you are though," he confirmed glancing around. "So I guess your assumption was kinda right." His eyes dropped to my lips. "I guess I owe Mo and Aunt Rach."

We stood there for a short while, neither of us saying much. The funny thing was, I felt like there was lots I wanted to say to Kane. Things that had been on my mind for the last few days. Words that hadn't left my lips.

For the life of me, I couldn't remember why I'd gotten so nervous when Kane had suggested we continue seeing each other when we were back in Iceland. Nor could I recall why I'd gotten equally anxious when we'd run each other once again.

"Do you mind if I walk with you through this exhibit?" he asked, breaking my thoughts.

I smiled, unable to help myself. "I don't mind one bit." Around us, folks moved in a wave of different paces, yet we kept in sync with one another.

His eyes studied mine. "Why does giving us a chance make you so nervous?"

As if that isn't the question of the whole damn year. Since meeting Kane, I'd been forced to come to terms with a lot of things I once hadn't taken the time to figure out. Therefore, I felt like I had to answer honestly.

"I think I'm finally starting to realize that my father leaving when I was young and my mother succumbing to alcoholism affected me more than I'd originally thought it did."

"How's so?" he asked.

I contemplated my answer, before speaking from the heart by telling him, "I used to think that as long as I was loyal, I'd never be like my father. On the other hand, if I was able to limit my alcohol intake to no more than two drinks when I went out socially, I'd never be like my mother."

"That makes sense," he said. "Children often look to their parents as people they either want to be like or people that they vow to never resemble ever in their life."

"True, but I'm slightly different where my mom is concerned. My mom was the type of woman that people never forgot. She was always the life of the party and even though I could recall almost every time I picked my mom off the floor after she'd drank too much, I also remembered the nights we'd spend watching our favorite movies and dancing to our favorite songs. She'd never wanted to be a mother, but she tried to do her best. When she got the news that she had liver cancer, it was a little too late for her to change her ways. Do you remember those Sailor Moon pajamas you saw me in?"

He nodded. "How could I forget? You looked adorable."

"Thanks," I said with a smile. "It was the last gift my mom got me so even though they don't fit anymore, I can't part with them. My aunt even started bringing them to the cleaners when I'd first moved in with her so that they wouldn't tear in her washing machine."

"Your aunt is really cool."

"She is."

"Is she your mom's sister?" he asked.

"Actually, she's my dad's sister. My mom didn't have any siblings and my father - wherever he is – is estranged from both me and my aunt. There's a few other relatives out there, but it's just me and Aunt Rach for the most part."

We came upon a booth selling peppermint hot chocolate and Kane got us both a cup as we dove into talking about his parents.

"So you aren't close to your dad?" I asked.

"Not really. He and my mom split when I was young and he moved out of state soon after. My sisters have better relationships with him than I do, but I've always been closer to my mom. Lately, my dad has been trying really hard to build our relationship and I'm finally letting him back in."

"Was the divorce your dad's fault?" I asked.

"You would think so based off how different I treat them, but I've learned that sometimes, there isn't a logical explanation for things. We may not ever be that close, but that doesn't mean I don't love him. But I also know life is short, so I'm thinking of popping up for a visit next month around Christmas. Honestly, I think he'd like you. My mom and sisters would too. If you're game, I'd love for you to meet them soon."

I took a sip of the warm drink and tried to hide my smile. I'd never had a man genuinely seem like he wanted me to meet his family. "Well, since you met Aunt Rach, then it only seems fair that I meet your family too."

"Then I'll set something up," he said.

When we reached the end of the art rooms, we both

froze. "Wow, we were so deep in our conversation, we didn't experience much."

"I'm glad we were able to talk, but let's go back through," he suggested. "Only this time, we'll stop at every room to get our money's worth."

I laughed. "That's right. We probably need to go through about five times for you to get two hundred dollars' worth of fun."

When I didn't hear him laugh along with me, I glanced his way and found his eyes low in observation. "Let's be clear about one thing," he stated. "I'd pay more than that if it meant I'd be able to spend some time getting to know you more."

It wasn't just his words that made the stone wall wrapped around my heart crack a little more. It was also the way he was looking at me, studying me in a way that made me feel like he truly saw me. He saw the Burgundy that wasn't putting on a façade, but rather, was being open in ways I never had before.

"I'm ready to give this a shot," I told him, earning me a look of surprise mixed with elation.

"Really?" he asked. "You're giving us the green light to date?" I nodded. "Well, in that case, let me be clear in telling you that I'm not a casual dating kind of guy. I date with a purpose and I think we'd be pretty damn good together if we gave a relationship a real shot."

I laughed out of nerves because, yeah, he was fine, but he was also *a lot* sometimes. "You lay it all out there, don't you?"

"You got to. If you don't make your stance clear, the next person waiting behind you in line is ready to capitalize off of your fuck up."

Shaking my head, I couldn't stop the smile from

creeping across my face. "There's no in-between with you either, is there?"

"See, now you're starting to get me." He placed his hand over his heart. "I'm touched."

I playfully pulled his hand away just as he reached for my forearm and pulled me closer to him. My arms wrapped around his neck, while his wrapped around my waist. The kiss we shared was soft. Light. It was almost as if he was teasing me since we were in public and couldn't kiss the way he wanted to kiss.

I wasn't sure when we'd started swaying to music that didn't exist, but we moved in unison, fellow art enthusiasts giving us thumbs up for reasons I wasn't sure of.

"I'm sure in your mind, you've only made me wait to properly date you for a week," he muttered. "Yet for me, it feels like I've been waiting since Iceland to get this response from you."

"In a way, you're wrong," I told him. "I don't know what this is between us, but I feel like it's been brewing since Iceland." And the daunting part was, I wasn't even nervous about opening myself up to him like I once was. In fact, I finally realized that he'd been peeling back my layers with every moment we'd shared.

CHAPTER 8

Burgundy

"*I*s that him?" Teegan asked when we arrived at the location of the new outdoor terrace and garden that Kane was working on. Ever since our impromptu date last Friday, I'd been seeing a lot of Kane.

Not only were we both working at Park Manor for the time being, but we'd also gone on two more dates since he'd shown up the other night. "Yeah, that's him."

"Damn, he sexy," Paityn said, smacking her lips. "You underestimated his looks B. He's kinda giving me mad Michael B Jordan vibes."

"Only sexier," Kathi added.

"And taller," Teegan supplied.

"And more rugged," Skylar said with a wink. "He's the one you met in Iceland, right?"

"Yep, one and the same." I'd briefed my girls on my

SHERELLE GREEN

trip months ago, but only earlier had I told them more
about Kane.

"I hear he's really talented," Kathi said. "I'm not
surprised he won the Park Manor bid."

"Me neither." With all of us looking his way, I tried
not to stare too hard at him as he discussed whatever
they had to do next with the rest of his team. I loved a
man in construction boots, washed out jeans, and a
white tee. He really was delicious to look at, but that
wasn't all he was. He had a good heart too and recently,
he'd shown me his portfolio and I'd noticed how
talented he really was.

"Oh shit, here he comes." I looked to the ladies. "Act
like we were out here to see the weather."

"Right," Teegan stated. "Because folks always come
outside to check the weather in the early evening after
being out all day."

I rolled my eyes. "I just meant, make yourselves look
like we aren't out here talking about him."

"As long as anything leaving your beautiful lips are
all good comments about me," he said as he
approached. "You can talk about me all you like." I
closed my eyes and mumbled a curse word as the others
laughed.

"I was just telling a few of the residents about your
project," I told him, introducing him to the others.
"They were curious how everything was going to look."

"Gotcha." He winked. "And here I was thinking my
girl was out here tryin' to show me off to her friends
when she thought I wasn't paying attention."

"Your assumption is more accurate," Paityn said.

Turning to her, I cracked my neck side to side and
shook my head. She shrugged which caused me to pop

my head again. We probably would have done that a couple more times had Kane not told me, "I missed you this morning," as he pulled me closer to him.

"I missed you too," I told him, right before he leaned down and placed a very X-rated kiss on my lips. PDA had never been my thing, but Kane didn't seem to care one bit. I was vaguely aware that my girls, as well as a couple of his employees, had grown quiet.

When he ended the kiss, I was sure I looked as dazed as I felt. "That was a nice greeting."

He grinned and leaned down to my ear. "If you thought that was nice, wait until you see what I have planned tonight."

I gasped knowing good and well his not-so-soft whisper had been overheard by my girls.

"Every kiss begins with Kane," Teegan sang as he walked away.

Sky shook her head. "You're so lame sometimes."

"It made B smile though," Teegan responded, directing her attention to me. "He called you his girl, so does that mean y'all are official?"

"I don't know," I told her honesty. "We haven't really had that talk yet, but I feel like it's kinda implied."

"Just make sure he doesn't have a record," Sky added, causing us all to look her way. "What? I'm just sayin'. When a man is that fine and that nice, has an amazing job with no wife, no kids, and no baby mama drama, you gotta ask the question. You can never be too careful in these streets."

I laughed harder than I had all day because Sky worked in law enforcement, so of course, she always had to warn us about possible crime or criminals. One of her anecdotes had me giving the side-eye to a ninety-five-year-old lady that frequented a grocery store that a lot of the Park Manor residents loved. Sky just knew that she was stealing baking supplies to make those cakes that she would sell to all of us by the slice. We'd all claimed there was no way Ms. Cooper was conning all of us into buying cake slices made with stolen ingredients until she was caught in the act. Granted, it wasn't the type of crime that any of us wanted to see her do time for, so we were glad when she only got community service. But Sky never let us forget that some of the best thieves dressed in sheep's clothing.

While Sky went on with her warnings, I stole another glance Kane's way and gasped when I noticed he was already staring at me. Since we'd reconnected, I'd told him I wanted to take things slow. But now, I was wondering why I'd ever suggested that in the first place. That look he was giving me mirrored the fire I was feeling for him too.

"Guess you don't need that dildo you purchased from me anymore, huh?" Paityn asked.

I laughed. "We aren't having sex yet."

"Sis please. Even if you aren't knocking boots, y'all will be soon.

"I told myself I needed to wait," I admitted. "He'd agreed to play by my rules, so we're waiting."

"Waiting for what?" she asked. "You've already had sex with him before."

I shrugged. "I know, but we're waiting for that perfect moment."

Just as the words left my mouth, Kane bent over to pick up a plant or something and my eyes went straight to his ass.

"Righttt," Paityn drawled. "Well, let me know how

that waiting thing goes because I predict you won't last until sunrise."

I laughed louder than was necessary. "Girl, I've gone years without sex before, so best believe I can go on our date tonight and keep it closed. I'm not that freaking weak."

* * *

YOU'RE SUCH A DAMN LIAR. Okay, so maybe I was being hard on myself, but the thought repeated in my mind several times this morning as I thought about the fact that we hadn't made it to the rest of our date. In fact, we hadn't made it past Kane's condo once we'd stopped to pick up some theater tickets he'd forgotten on his dresser.

Since we'd had some time to spare, it made sense for me to come up to his place and check it out. He was fantastic at landscaping, but Kane wasn't too bad with interior design either. However, the thing he was the best at? Making me moan his name in ecstasy.

Except now, it was morning and although he was still asleep, I'd awakened in a slight panic since I hadn't woken up with a man since that night we'd shared in Iceland. Not only did I need to take a shower, but my breath was funky and my normally chic bob was plastered onto the side of my face. I wanted to slip out of the bed elegantly, yet every time I moved, Kane pulled me closer to him in his sleep.

After several failed attempts, I was finally able to not-so-gracefully slide out of the bed and onto the floor. From there, I figured the best option was to crawl to the en suite bathroom which would have been a great idea had Kane not woken up and caught me with me crawling.

"And to think I'd imagined you on your knees in this very bedroom," he mumbled, still half asleep. "Except I didn't think you'd be trying to escape."

"I'm not leaving," I explained. "I just wanted to take a shower and didn't want to wake you."

"I was awake the minute you started fidgeting in bed an hour ago."

"Seriously!" I squealed, finally standing. "You knew I was on the struggle bus and was probably trying to make my way to the bathroom, yet you just played sleep?"

Instead of responding to me, his eyes went up and down my body, the fire in them evident. Rarely, did I walk around butt ass naked, but I was comfortable with my body, so he could look all he wanted. The bedsheet was covering his rising dick, but I could see the imprint and immediately, my mouth began to water thinking of all the dirty things we did last night.

"I'm going to take a shower," I announced, needing to take advantage of the fact that he was half asleep. Otherwise, he'd be my morning distraction just like he'd been last night. Typical Kane, he didn't give a shit about my announcement, but instead, was out of the bed in seconds and pulling us both back onto the duvet.

"I really need to take a shower," I pleaded.

"I like you a little ripe," he teased. "Especially when I'm the cause." His fingers slid from my stomach to my throbbing clit, his thumb moving in circles that made me pant in want.

"Kane, why don't you shower with me," I suggested.

"Absolutely," he agreed. "Right after I do this." His lips landed on my breasts, his tongue swirling around my sensitive nipples. I'd always been a fan of foreplay, yet with Kane, I was realizing that my patience level was shot to shit.

Every time we laid in bed together, all I could think about was how soon he'd be inside me. He was an addiction I never saw coming. A reminder that I was *all* woman and owed it to myself not to let certain feelings and emotions stay dormant for years.

It didn't take long before his lips and hands on my body made me explode in a pleasurable release I felt from the top of my head to the tips of my toes. I'd still been coming down from my high when he got a condom from his dresser and returned to bed.

His eyes held mine as his dick slid past my folds, the moment more intense than anything else he'd done this morning. Someone should have told him that I hated eye contact when having sex. Or at least, I used to hate it. It used to feel like other men thought that eye contact was something women wanted and when they came, I was forced to look at nothing but their faces. Not my favorite.

With Kane, everything was different. His was a face I looked forward to seeing every day. When we locked eyes as he thrusted inside me, our chemistry reached levels of no return. We hadn't talked too much about what would happen with us, but some things didn't need words. Sometimes, two people were on the same page without a deep conversation needing to take place. I knew we still had lots to learn about each other, but in time, I was sure all those talks would happen naturally.

When he twisted me slightly to my side bringing him deeper into my core, my moans echoed off the walls, the orgasm I knew would follow teasing me with convulsions.

"You're beautiful," he whispered, increasing his tempo. I wanted to tell him that he made me feel more beautiful than I'd ever felt. Yet, my mouth and mind weren't cooperating at the moment. My thoughts soon ceased to nothing but Kane and the way he was making me feel. It was clear he wasn't taking a break anytime soon, so I guessed our shower would have to wait.

CHAPTER 9

Kane

Things with Burgundy were going better than expected and after only three weeks, I was hooked in the best way possible. Work had been pretty busy for her and I was trying to wrap up a couple projects at Park Manor so surprisingly, we didn't see each other as much as we'd liked. Still, ending the night with her had become my favorite time of the day.

Yet, the message I'd gotten today was a reminder that we still had some important things to discuss with each other. And although all I wanted to do at the moment was head to her office and take her to lunch to talk, I was spending my off day at Park Manor for another reason entirely.

I knocked on the door when I reached the condo that matched the number in the text message I'd received earlier. She answered right away. "I'm sorry," she said. "I wasn't sure who else to call."

"It's okay," I told her, stepping into her condo. "I'm glad you called me. What can I do to help?"

She wrapped her arms around her shoulders and sighed. "It just seems like no matter how hard I try, I can't seem to get over everything that has happened."

"I'm sorry you're having such a hard time with this," I said honestly.

"There was once a time when you loved me, right?"

I sighed. "Of course there was, but like I told you before, it's always been in more of a good friend kind of way. I'm with Burgundy now and things are serious between us."

"More serious than we were?" she asked.

"Yes, if you want a direct answer," I told her. "Listen, you and I will always be friends, but I assumed from your message that you called me here because you needed help with something."

She glanced at me, tears rimming her eyelids. "I feel like there's no one in the world who would give two shits about me if I were gone tomorrow."

"I would and you know that." I motioned for her to follow me onto her couch. "What can I do to help you through this?"

She sighed. "I've thought about seeking professional help again. Depression isn't something to mess with and I know the signs because I've been here before."

On the outside looking in, it seemed as though she had a good life. However, I'd gotten pretty close to her over the years and had learned that her life wasn't at all how it appeared to be. I'd never been able to ignore a friend when I noticed them struggling and I'd made a promise to look after her even if it complicated my life more than I wanted.

"I'm really not trying to be a thorn in your side," she said. "Especially since you're in a new relationship. Have you even told her about our past?"

I shook my head. "Not yet, but I will. We're still kinda fresh, so I was trying to give our relationship some time to grow first. But I don't want you concerned about that. Right now, let's focus on the next steps we need to take to get you back on track."

She smiled for the first time since I'd arrived. "You're the best, Kane. I don't know what I'd do without you. Burgundy is lucky to have a man like you in her life."

I smiled back, but mine was a little more forced. Her words were kind, but I didn't mistake for one second that her presence could be more of a complication with my relationship with Burgundy than I was prepared for.

* * *

Burgundy

"ARE YOU SURE IT WAS HIM?" I asked Teegan.

She nodded. "I'm pretty sure. I saw Kane hug her right outside her condo. It looked like he was leaving her place."

I paced my office, my heels clicking on the wood floor echoing my annoyance. Technically, Kane didn't owe me any explanations. Yet, I knew deep down that I needed him to explain why he'd spent his off day in another woman's home.

"I knew he was too good to be true."

Teegan shook her head. "Don't do that. Don't assume the worst when you haven't talked to him yet. There could be an explanation as to why he was with her."

"Or they could be fucking," I stated plainly. "He's charming. Good-looking. I've noticed tenants looking at him even if they've heard he and I are dating. So honestly, he doesn't owe me shit."

"But he does though," she said. "Just because you haven't said the words making it an official relationship, you're committed to him and from what I've seen, he doesn't act like a man who isn't committed to you. Any chance Kane gets, he's kissing you or hugging you. Whenever I run into him in the hallway, he's anxious to tell me about something fun you both did on a date or asking me questions about how we met."

"I said he was charming," I reminded. "Never took him for the player type, but he wouldn't be the first man to lie about having a secret relationship."

"I've seen the look of a man who's being unfaithful and Kane isn't it. The only reason I'm telling you about what I saw is because you're my girl and I felt like you should know." I opened my mouth to respond, but was interrupted.

"Did you hear the news?" Colin asked, bursting into my office without knocking.

"Colin, can't you tell I'm busy?"

"Sorry." He sat down next to Teegan anyway. "Just figured you'd want to know in case you haven't heard."

"Heard what?" I asked.

"Larry's been fired," he said. "He's with management right now, but from what I've heard, it's not looking too good for him."

I looked to Teegan who pretended to act surprised. "Did you know about this?" I asked her.

She shrugged. "Some of the residents may or may not have reached out to someone who was able to dig up some information about Larry's past job and the fact that he's been known to discriminate against race. With everything going on in the world today, places are acting more promptly to nip that stuff in the bud. If he didn't want to be questioned by management, he should have been a better individual."

I shook my head. "Have I ever told you that I'm glad you and the other OG Park Manor residents are on my side?"

She smiled. "Nope, but glad to know you appreciate us. And I have a feeling that property manager position is yours if you want it."

"Of course it's hers," Colin said. "She's the best person for the job. Without Burgundy, this place wouldn't function at all."

My eyes widened in surprise. "I always thought you couldn't stand me?"

He laughed. "More like you always lumped me with the rest of these assholes and I've always wanted to fit in, so I just played along. But I've never liked how they treated you and I've gone on record with HR several times to tell them how I felt like you were wrongfully treated."

"You're lying," I said. "There's no way you did that. You and I barely talked."

He raised his hands in the air. "That was what you wanted, not me. I'm not one to force a friendship."

"And how am I supposed to know you aren't just saying all this stuff so that I don't fire you the first chance I get."

He laughed. "Trust me, I'm being honest. But if you want to let me go, it's not like you won't have reason to. I'm a slow learner sometimes and it's taken me a while to get the hang of my job here. You may not have liked me, but you were the only one who took time to try and help me out."

"That's because you were making us look bad," I said with a laugh. "If I wasn't worried that Park Manor would be hurt because of your mess ups, I wouldn't have helped at all."

"I don't believe that for one minute," he said. "You care a lot more than you let on and I've known that about you since I started working here."

Well, damn. I never would have thought there was more to Colin than what met the eye, but he was surprising me.

"I'll let you get back to what you were doing," he stated.

"Thank you for letting me know what's going on," I told him. "Oh, and Colin. One last thing," I said, right before he'd reached the door.

"Yes?"

I squinted before asking him, "Did you honestly work on President Obama's campaign?"

He laughed. "Have you wondered that since I started working here?"

I nodded. "Pretty much."

"Yes, I did. Best eight years of my career yet. But I

learned I wasn't built for politics, so after his presidency ended, I decided to try other avenues, which led me to Park Manor."

"Ah, I see. Thanks for telling me."

"Anytime."

After he left the office, I found myself having a newfound respect for Colin. "Who knew he had layers."

"He's never been as bad as you make him out to be," Teegan said. "And now that you're in charge, you'll make a lot of positive changes here."

"I'm not in charge yet," I reminded her.

"You basically are," she countered, her eyes growing with concern. "Have you decided if you're going to approach Kane about what I saw?"

"You already know I am," I told her. "I'm not about to be out here looking like a fool. Especially if I get a promotion. I already feel like a lot of eyes are already on me."

"Who cares what others think," she said. "Talk to him because you want to figure out what's going on, but not just because you're concerned with what the residents will think if he's stepping out on you."

I nodded. "No worries, I'm approaching him for me and me only." And I prayed to God that he had a good explanation for being in another woman's condo in the middle of the damn day.

CHAPTER 10

Kane

*W*hen I'd gotten the message to meet Burgundy at her aunt's house, my gut was telling me that something was wrong. I wasn't the type to overanalyze a text, but hers had lacked emotion and for the past couple days, she'd made up excuses as to why we couldn't see each other. By the time I knocked on her aunt's door, that feeling hadn't subsided.

"Come in," she said, stepping aside for me to enter. I leaned in for a kiss, but she gave me her cheek. *Yeah, something is definitely up.* I just wanted her to tell me what I'd done so I could just apologize for it and salvage some of what I was sure would be a long night.

"My aunt is out for the night, so we can talk freely in the living room."

I took a seat across from where she'd sat, glancing

around a bit. "From what I can see, the place looks really nice."

"Thanks," she said, eyeing me curiously. "And I'm sure you're wondering why I've been avoiding you."

I nodded. "Yeah, I am because it seemed like things between us were going great, then suddenly, you're keeping communication short and blunt."

"I'll just come out and say it." She sighed. "Teegan saw you leave Hazel's condo and she said you looked very cozy. So what was that about? Are you fucking Hazel?"

Shit. I should have assumed this had something to do with Hazel. "No, I'm not fucking her."

"Were you fucking her before we met?" she asked.

I squeezed the bridge of my nose. "Okay, so this is not how I wanted to have this conversation, but yes, I've slept with Hazel before."

She frowned. "And you didn't feel a need to tell me that you'd had sex with someone who lived in Park Manor after everything I told you."

"That was wrong of me," I admitted. "But you have to understand that she and I were never like that. Hazel has suffered from depression for as long as I've known her. She never had a chance to meet her parents and when her grandfather passed away, others in her life had to take her under our wings."

"How long ago were you two together?" she asked.

"Over eight years ago," I told her. "We were young and it only happened once after I finally told my pops that I'd take her on a date. He'd always had a soft spot for Hazel. She was like a granddaughter to him. And she's been in several relationships since me. We didn't get that serious, but Hazel is the type to latch on to folks.

"When we'd had sex, it was after her grandfather had passed and I'd known that she needed a release. She needed to forget what had happened. We never even went on a date after that night, but our friendship grew."

I could read the emotions darting across Burgundy's face. I hated that she had to find out about Hazel the way she did, but a part of me was relieved that it was out in the open.

"I won't pretend like seeing her won't make me cringe knowing that she's seen you naked."

"If it makes you feel any better, Hazel actually won't be living there for much longer," I told her.

"How come?"

"She'll be reaching out to you soon to let you know she's placing her condo on sale. She experienced another death of someone close to her, so her depression has hit an all-time high. She's never dealt with death well. That's why she called me. Her episodes are getting worse, so I'm going to assist her in getting the help she needs. Pops had already found some great places, so I'm making my way down the list to find the best."

"Your grandfather seems like a good man."

"Was a good man," I corrected. "But that's a matter of opinion. Personally, I loved the dude. Yet, from what I've heard, you couldn't stand him and thought he didn't deserve to work at Park Manor."

Her mouth dropped. "Oh, crap. Buddy was your grandfather?"

"Not biologically, but like Hazel, he was friends with my grandfather. The three of them grew up together, but I actually hadn't gotten a chance to meet my grandfather. So Pops, or Buddy as you know him, kinda took me in as his own. The only thing about Pops was that he seemed to surround himself with people who were like family, but I've never actually met anyone who really was family."

"That's unusual," she said.

"It was at first, but I got used to it. Clearly, he has family somewhere because I was all prepared to pay for the funeral, yet, the funeral home informed me that family had already paid for it. Funny thing was, I didn't meet anyone that day who I didn't already know."

"So how did he die?" she asked.

"I'm not sure and honestly, I'll probably never know since an autopsy wasn't done."

She grew quiet, before saying, "I feel bad that I never knew any of this about him."

"That was Pops' nature," I explained. "I'm not sure anyone ever really knew him, but I'd like to think that my grandfather and Hazel's were the ones who knew the real Pops. To me, he was my surrogate grandfather and when I have kids, I'll tell them all about him just like I would my biological grandfather."

"Our lives seem connected in the strangest ways," she said. "Did you know who I was in Iceland?"

I shook my head. "No, I didn't know you. Pops never mentioned your name specifically to me and I had only been in Park Manor a couple times before landing the contract. But when I was at Hazel's the other day, she said that the two of you didn't get along and one day, you even pulled her aside to ask her if she was okay when you caught him leaving her place."

"Yeah, I didn't like how often he was in there, but now that I know about Hazel's relationship to Buddy, it all makes more sense now."

"I can't believe he's gone sometimes," I admitted. "Since we weren't blood and he was such a private man, he died with me having more questions than answers."

"I don't remember seeing you at the memorial," she noted.

"I wasn't there. By the time Park Manor had the memorial, I was off the grid in Switzerland trying to accept what had happened. Life is unpredictable and although I thought I'd be prepared for most things, I hadn't been prepared for that. I'd just done a lot of self-reflecting by the time we met in Iceland."

Her eyes softened. "I'm sorry he passed away and I'm even more sorry that I seem to have misjudged him. At least now it makes sense why he was so hard to read. According to you, that was just Buddy."

"It was, but Pops wasn't a saint. He had faults just like anyone else. Everything you felt was probably valid."

"Ah, sort of," she admitted. "I was kinda harsh on him, but it's nice knowing all this now."

"From now on, let's be honest in our relationship no matter what the circumstance," I suggested.

She smiled. "Is that what this is? A relationship?"

"Do you want to have that whole Facebook official talk?" I asked, laughing. "Or maybe you're one of those women who rather start posting pics of us on Instragram and Snapchat?"

She shook her head. "Nah, I'm good on all of that. As long as we agree to be committed to one another, that's good enough for me."

"I agree," I said. "Besides, I've been calling you my girlfriend now for weeks."

"Is that so?" Her smile grew wider. "When were you gonna tell me?"

I laughed. "Just now. No more secrets between us, then?"

"No more secrets," she agreed, before she began to look guilty.

"What's that look for?"

"Nothing too serious, but if we're being honest, there's something…quite a bit I want to update you on." She glanced around the living room. "Can we move this to the kitchen so I can make us some chamomile tea?"

"Sure," I told her without hesitation. She seemed nervous about whatever she wanted to tell me, but no matter what it was, I hoped she knew there was nothing that could stop me from continuing to fall for her.

* * *

Burgundy

"Good news first?" I asked him after I'd made us both some tea.

"Give it to me."

I took a deep breath. "This morning, management officially called me and offered me the position of Property Manager for Park Manor."

"That's amazing," he said, placing a quick peck on my lips. "But I can't say I'm surprised. You're great at what you do and everyone at Park Manor loves you. Management clearly knows that."

I beamed. "Aww, thank you. I'm really excited and

of course, I accepted their offer. I even told them the real reason Larry had fired me in the first place before he hired me back and they still offered me the position."

"I'm not sure I even know the reason you got let go," he stated.

"You don't." I ran my finger over the rim of my mug. "But that's the other thing I wanted to tell you."

"You don't have to tell me anything you aren't ready to tell me."

I shook my head. "You said no secrets and I agree, no secrets. I didn't just get let go because I didn't have a degree. He let me go because he'd found out that I didn't get my GED until I had already been working at Park Manor for a year."

I braced myself for him to be surprised or maybe see a hint of disappointment in his eyes. Instead, I was met with a look of confusion as he asked, "Is that it? You were nervous to tell me that you got your GED later than some?"

"Well, yeah," I said. "Education is a big deal and when my mom got sick, school wasn't a priority. I wanted to make lasting memories with her and kind of lost my way for a while. Then, when Aunt Rach stepped in, we worked on building our relationship and she didn't push me. I may have lied on my Park Manor application, but I knew I could do that job."

He was so quiet that it started to get a little eerie. I couldn't read the look on his face and I'd just told him a secret that not many knew. "Do you think less of me?" I asked, although I wasn't sure I could handle his response.

He took my hand into his, his comfort soothing my rattled nerves. "I don't think less of you," he told me. "If anything, I think you're the strong, selfless woman that I've known since we've met. Taking care of your mom at a young age couldn't have been easy and watching her deteriorate a little more each day must have been even harder. Yet, you put her needs before your own and still managed to excel in life."

"Thank you for saying that."

"I meant every word," he said. I studied his eyes, soaking in all the admiration I saw in them. I didn't know where the hell Kane had come from, but I was grateful that I'd been given the chance to know him.

"Do you find it weird that our paths never crossed before?" I asked.

He shook his head. "Not at all. We weren't meant to meet all those times before. Our time hadn't come yet and our tracks weren't meant to cross until Iceland."

I smiled. "I've never met a man who believed in fate the way you do."

"You don't think the fact that Pops' memorial was the moment you decided to think about your impact on the world was a coincidence, do you? Or that you met me a few weeks later after this revelation?"

I thought about his questions, determining that, "I don't think it was a coincidence either."

Soon, the tea was long forgotten as Kane pulled me to him and placed the softest kiss on my lips that I'd ever had. It was sweet. *Perfect.* A promise that from this point on, I had him in my corner. A man who recognized the truth in my heart and the past pain in my eyes, but pushed past my protective barriers to help me learn to trust without restrictions.

Before, he was just a stranger with good intentions. Strong in his somewhat unusual beliefs, but the best distraction I could have had at the time. Now that I truly knew the amazing man he was, I couldn't help but think about this whole destiny concept in a new light. I couldn't stop my heart from pounding so loudly, that I had no choice but to stop blocking my blessings. And with the way Kane's playful tongue dipped into my ready mouth and turned our sweet kiss into naughty foreplay, *this* was definitely a blessing.

EPILOGUE

 *hree months later…*

Burgundy

"Are you sure about this?" I asked.

Kane shook his head. "Baby, how many times are you going to ask me that question?"

"I just want to be sure," I told him. "I can be a lot to handle sometimes and moving in together is a big step."

"A big step that I'm more than ready to make," he said, taking my hand in his. "B, I've been waiting to move in with you since the first time I dropped you off at your aunt's. Baby, we've been ready for this next step and honestly, there's no backing out now anyway." He nodded to the others in the room.

Our real estate agent, Nash, was already nodding his head in agreement. "He's right. Typically, couples have this conversation before the day we close."

I laughed. "We've had this conversation plenty of times. I guess I'm just being extra careful."

"Too careful," Kane said. "Now, let's finish all this paperwork so we can get the keys to our first home together."

I squealed. "Eeek. This is insane, but yeah, let's finish up."

A couple hours later, we were official homeowners and I was beaming from ear to ear. Since I'd passed on moving back into Park Manor, we'd spent most of our time at Kane's place, but since he was renting, he'd suggested buying a place.

We weren't engaged or anything, but I was pretty damn sure I would be spending the rest of my life with him, so getting a home together just felt right. And even though I'd thought Kane was insane for recruiting some of our friends and family to help us move some items into our new home before the movers we'd hired over the weekend did the heavy lifting, I had to admit it was a pretty nice first day.

"This place is dope," Paityn said. "So proud of y'all."

"I particularly like some of the artwork Kane has," Teegan chimed in.

"And it's nice and big enough for a family," Kathi added with a wink.

Skylar glanced around. "I'm still trying to figure out what's the best spare bedroom because I *will* be crashing at your place."

Some loud banging at the door got our attention. "Damn, am I the only mothafucka moving shit?" Mo grumbled, struggling with a couple of heavy boxes.

Kane shook his head before heading over to help

him move everything, while I helped Aunt Rach unpack the box of dishes. I'd gotten even closer to Mo and had gotten a chance to meet Kane's parents and his sisters last month when Kane had invited them all into town.

Immediately, I clicked with his mom and sisters, so I wasn't surprised they were all extremely close. His dad had taken a little longer for me to warm up to, but it was only because he seemed like the type of man who kept his thoughts and feelings to himself, so you never really knew what he was thinking. I was similar in that way, so it hadn't bothered me at all.

"He's good for you," Aunt Rach said when were semi-alone in the kitchen. "And I know I've said this to you before, but he was a change in your life that you needed."

"I guess I won't trade him in for a new model," I teased. "Plus, we just bought this house together so we're committed more now than we ever have been."

"Knowing Kane, a ring will follow soon," she said. "You know that boy is always trying to do things when you least expect it."

"I told him I don't like surprises, but he can't help himself."

"Burgundy, let that boy surprise you all he wants. It'll help keep your relationship fresh."

I giggled. "Duly noted, auntie."

Everybody made quick work of helping us unpack the few things we had and I couldn't recall a time I'd been happier than I'd felt now. Almost ten months ago, I'd set out on a mission to figure out what legacy I would leave, and my gut had told me that Park Manor would have a huge part in that. What I hadn't known was that Park Manor wouldn't be the only factor to impact me, but also my aunt, my friends, and my man. Because yes, Kane was my man and I was too damn excited that I had him by my side. Life was looking pretty damn good and for the first time in years, I felt like everything was right in my little world.

* * *

Kane

"OUR FIRST NIGHT in our new home," I said aloud as Burgundy and I got cozy on the air mattress we'd set up in the living room. We didn't have our bed set yet, but it hadn't mattered to us.

After feeling like I never needed to place roots anywhere, I'd finally found a woman who made me feel like home was wherever she was. So, if my girl wanted to stay in California, well damnit, we were staying in the golden state.

"And our first meal," she added, taking a bite of the pizza we'd ordered. I waited until we'd both finished eating before I took out an envelope and handed it to her.

"What's this?" she asked.

"I'm not sure," I goaded. "Could be our first bill, or it could be plane tickets?"

She squealed. "Oh my God, where are we going?" Before I could even answer, she was ripping open the envelope and yelling even louder. "We're going to Africa? Oh shit, are you for real? I've always wanted to go to Africa."

"I know," I said with a laugh. "You've only told more times than I can count." I'd been to Africa several times, but I was sure going with Burgundy was going to top all of it. Plus, it was a huge continent, so there were lots of places I still wanted to visit.

"This is unreal," she squeaked. "I pray that these tickets aren't fake."

"I'm offended. You know I don't play when it comes to trips. Of course these tickets are real."

Suddenly, she stopped squealing.

"What's wrong?" I asked.

"Are you proposing in Africa?" she blurted. "Is that why we're going on this impromptu trip?"

Shit. Well, yeah. Of course I was proposing in Africa! What man wouldn't take his woman to the homeland and not propose. But I wasn't telling her any of that, so instead, I acted quick on my feet and told her, "Although you know I can't wait to marry you, I have to go Africa for a landscaping job. I thought you would love to go with me. Remember that development group who visited Park Manor last month to see all the new updates?"

"The one who mentioned building atriums for some of their establishments?" she asked.

"Yeah, that group. Well, I was talking to their president and it turns out, one of the buildings is in Africa. A resort I think. It's brand new and they asked me to be on the project."

She started squealing again. "Oh my God baby, that's amazing. I'm so proud of you." She scooted closer to me and held my gaze.

"Well show me then," I said, pulling her to me. When she opened her mouth to probably say something sassy, I shut her up with a kiss that was just as sensual as our kisses always were.

This is the life, I thought for the hundredth time today. Pops was right. I'd always been running toward something, I just hadn't found it... until I'd met Burgundy Anderson. I'd changed her, but she'd changed me more and if I was right about fate, life was looking pretty damn good in our future.

"That was amazing," she said, when we came up for air. "And I can't wait to go to Africa. Sorry about asking if you were proposing there, but it just came out. I'm trying to get better at surprises. Aunt Rach even said that—"

I silenced her with another kiss, hoping she thought I just couldn't get enough of her tonight. Truth was, kissing Burgundy was my favorite pastime. But *damn*, she'd thrown a monkey wrench in my plans by guessing I'd propose in Africa. So now, I needed to come up with a new strategy. If she kept talking about Africa, my face would give it away that she'd ruined my idea and I didn't want that disappointment weighing heavy on her heart. Therefore, kissing her quiet seemed like the best option.

A couple minutes later, I was horny as hell, but I had a new plan, a new goal, and a new location where I would propose to Burgundy.

I just hoped she was up for cave diving.

WOULD LOVE TO HEAR FROM YOU!

I hope you enjoyed Her Undeniable Attraction! I love to hear from readers! Thanks in advance for any reviews, messages or emails :).

Also, stop by my online Coffee Corner and get the latest info on my books, contests, events and more!

www.bit.ly/SherelleGreensCoffeeCorner

Save and Author! Leave a Review!

WOMEN OF PARK MANOR

Each novella in the Women of Park Manor series can be read in any order. See below for a list of all the books in the series.

FAKE NEWS

Her

Investigative Reporter Rule #1: Never get too close to the subject of your story. Up until now, I've been able to separate business from real life. Yet, the more up close and personal I get to him, the more difficult it is for me to back away. With each penetrating stare, he sucks me in deeper. His kisses are as lethal as his words. He has secrets that could cost me my job and put me in danger. So why do I feel like he's dangerous for all the right reasons.

Him

Street Fighter Rule #1: Never underestimate your opponent. I don't know much about her, so I definitely shouldn't trust her. She has me opening up in ways I've never done with anyone. Steering clear of her at all costs should be my goal. Yet with each conversation, I uncover more layers. She's hiding something. Then again, so am I. The more I'm with her, the harder I fall. Now I need to figure out if I'm the one putting her life at jeopardy, or is she the one risk I never saw coming.

EXCERPT: FAKE NEWS

"Never fuck up the first impression. You only get one chance."
~ Steel ~

Destiny

The hidden details always tell the story one wants to keep secret. I thought back to something one of my substitute English teachers told me back in high school the day before she took her own life. It rocked my small, Illinois hometown because people in my town didn't do tragic shit. Yeah, tragedies happened, but if a person died, it was usually from a car accident or old age. Never at their own hand.

To be honest, I never cared for her as a substitute because I loved our regular teacher who had gone on maternity leave at the time. The substitute was kinda young and her teaching style was far from traditional. Back then, I didn't like too much change. However, her class began to grow on me after a while. She even tried convincing me to be a reporter for the school newspaper and I declined. That is, until news hit the high school of her passing.

I became immersed in the fact that so many of us knew so little about her. She didn't have much family. Didn't have many friends. Yet, I'd snuck into her temporary office at school that same fateful day and uncovered things about her that I never would have guessed.

For instance, her favorite green vegetable was peas. *Peas*. Rarely did anyone pass up broccoli or green beans for peas. So, naturally, I kept digging after that, and found out that she'd been married once to an asshole who cheated on her and married a close friend. *Triflin' ass*. According to Facebook, her ex had three kids with that bitch now.

Another thing I found out was that she was an award-winning violinist and had published three books under a pen name. She only became a teacher after marrying her ex. I couldn't be certain, but my gut told me she gave up her dreams for him. It only took a little more digging for me to figure out that I was right. She had.

As I searched through all her private memories, baffled that no one from the high school or the police had walked in on me yet, I was struck with a thought that rocked my fifteen-year-old mind at the time.

Why had no one come into the office since we'd gotten the news this morning? Why was her office still unlocked? Why hadn't they canceled school after we heard the news?

The truth was like eating a rotten apple. Bitter. Full of bacteria. Disgusting. The school and police discarded her death the same way the town had dismissed her the entire time she lived there filling in for our teacher. And to top it off, her name was Sarah Smith. Sarah *fucking* Smith. Something so simple it was easy for folks to forget that she was a human being with real emotions and a life that deserved to be celebrated.

So I finally took Ms. Smith's advice and joined our school newspaper. After three months, I still couldn't get the teacher who moderated the paper and our principle to agree to let me write an article about Ms. Smith's legacy. When I heard my twenty-fourth no, I quit the paper and started my own blog instead. It was on that blog that I shared her story, which eventually got picked up by a popular Midwest newspaper.

Her story wasn't special, but it also wasn't unimportant either. She deserved to be remembered, and when I found out that her whack ass ex-husband and that homewrecker she called a friend deleted all their social media pages, I considered my job done. Ms. Smith would have been proud.

I guess, in a way, I never forgot about that teacher because she was right. I fell in love with reporting after that. No story was too small and no topic was off limits, even if that meant doing something a little less safe like I was for my current story.

"Come on, Destiny. You got this," I said to myself as I walked down the cool, dark hallway, my three-inch peach heels clicking to the beat of the latest techno hip-hop flavored song. I truly disliked techno anything. Especially when they used those stupid beats to fuck up a perfectly good song.

I adjusted the sleek, black eye mask I was given at the door upon entering the once abandoned warehouse. After waiting over six months to get an invite to the underground fight club, my contact had finally pulled through.

Following the sound of the music, I took note of the groups of people going in and out several rooms with flashing dance lights and light fog floating at the base of the floor. Soon, the music was a mix of hip hop and R&B, the vibe slightly changing.

Peeking into one of the rooms, I wasn't surprised by the sloppy dancing and drunken state of the attendees. *Is this a fight club or a get-your-freak-on party?* I wasn't sure what this part of the warehouse was for, but I also didn't have time to figure it out now.

I'd been working for an online magazine for a couple years and was loving every minute of it. Especially since I was on the rise to become one of their best investigative reporters. Nothing ever stood in the way of a story, and before I left tonight, I would be one step closer to finding out how this operation worked and confirm that the fight club was allowing attendees to illegitimately bet on fighters in one of the biggest illegal gambling rings southern Cali had ever seen.

Edging slowly around a corner just past the dance rooms, I walked up to a table with a man and woman collecting money.

"That will be thirty-five dollars," the redheaded girl said, smacking her gum a little too loudly.

"But we'll knock off ten bucks for you," said the green-eyed guy who couldn't take his eyes off my chest.

"No, we can't," the redhead retorted as she slapped the guy across the back of the head. "It's thirty-five dollars. No discounts."

"No need. I'm filling in for Amanda for the next few

weeks. She's out of town." *More like, she was never coming back according to my source, but that wasn't any of their business.*

The redhead looked me up and down. "You can't possibly be filling in for our best girl."

Ouch. "Well I am, so I would appreciate it if you pointed me in the direction of your boss." I subconsciously ran my fingers through my thick, curly, brown hair with honey blonde highlights in attempt to smooth out any unruly strands. Usually, I would ignore a woman like the redhead. But tonight, I was out of my element. I was wearing a tight ass black mini skirt and black crop top, which was the typical attire for a female working for the Enclave Fight Club, one of the top fight clubs in L.A.

And even though it shouldn't have mattered, my hair hadn't turned out the way I wanted it to. Last night, I rodded my curly hair instead of letting it air dry to change up the style of my natural afro-curls. Before I put on my Enclave uniform, I'd just thrown my hair in a ponytail, furthering my annoyance with not being as prepared tonight as I would have liked. Nonetheless, I needed to play the part of a badass bitch and work the fighting ring like any other girl hired for the position.

"The office is back that way." The guy pointed to another hallway.

"Thanks," I said as I made my way to the office. I ignored the fact that I could feel the eyes of the green-eyed blond pinned to my ass. I'd been blessed with a little too much junk in the trunk, something that only seemed to grow when I didn't work out on the regular.

Although I was glad that my love for food hadn't caught up with me in all areas of my body yet, I'd always admired the beauty in the many different shapes and sizes of women. My passion for fashion, hair, and beauty attracted the love of over three-hundred thousand YouTube followers who tuned into my station to hear my alter ego discuss the latest beauty products, hairstyles, and fashion trends.

As I approached a closed door with a small glass window, I felt a chill go down my spine. Getting this far meant I definitely wasn't turning back. I knocked a couple times, unsure if anyone was actually in the office. The entire warehouse was pretty dark and I assumed they preferred it that way for the underground fighting.

Hearing the loud clatter of a locker closing, I shifted my head to the side. I could feel someone standing there observing me, but I couldn't see their face. It was even more unsettling that I couldn't even make out the shadow of the person whose face had just vacated the locker. After a few seconds, the office door swung open, regaining my attention.

"You must be Amanda's replacement," the tall, burly man said as he stuck out his hand to greet me. He appeared to be in his mid to upper thirties, but I wasn't sure.

"Yes, that's me." I accepted his firm handshake, noticing that he was the first person I saw who wasn't wearing a mask and concealing his identity. Although the masks represented a sense of mystery and excitement, the fact that the owner wasn't wearing one meant he didn't give a shit if anyone knew who he was. *Interesting.*

"Good." He ushered me into the office and pointed to an X on the floor. "Stand here so I can get a good view of your overall look."

I only hesitated for a second. He wasn't the warm,

fuzzy type, but I couldn't mess up this investigation. That didn't mean I didn't feel strange to go into somewhat of an interview and have my body be my main selling qualification. It baffled me even more to think of how many women and men probably had to stand in this exact spot and get cross-examined.

Instead of glancing at the floor, I watched the brawny man as he observed me closely. I was put at ease when I realized that he actually appeared to be observing me just like a designer would a model. I welcomed his disinterest because it made the situation less unnerving.

I stood tall, not letting any insecurities seep through. Standing at five-nine, I didn't look anything like the norm of Enclave. Big, afro-curly hair. Smooth, coffee brown skin. I was the opposite of blond-haired Amanda who I was replacing. Therefore, he shocked the hell out of me when he said, "You look great. Probably one of the most striking girls we have on staff. The crowd will love your look."

He gave me a quick half-smile before his scowl returned as he handed me a couple sheets of paper stapled in the left corner. "Review this contract and get it back to me before our meeting tomorrow. Staff meets at 6 p.m., and don't forget to wear your mask. With the exception of me, everyone has to wear his or her mask at all times, including fighters. Attendees get masks as well, but it's up to them if they keep them on."

"Why do we wear masks?" I asked even though I had an idea.

"The masks add a sense of mystery to the Enclave team," he explained. "It makes us different than other fight clubs, and customers really love that."

"Understood." I took the papers from him and placed them in my bag.

"Here's a key to your locker. Number A16." He handed me a wristlet key. "Everyone calls me Steel. What name do you go by?"

I thought about the fact that my YouTube personality name was Dese Nicole, and my investigative journalist name was Cecilia Blackwell. But my legal birth name was Destiny Karen Nicole Jennings thanks to my parents who wanted to give me the middle name of both my grandmothers. So I chose the nickname that I'd always wished would catch on when I was a kid, but never did.

"DK … Everyone calls me DK."

"Well, DK, you're up in ten minutes. The crowd needs to get used to seeing a new face, so we'll have you holding the signs for the rounds today. Someone will be there to direct you when it's time. Good luck, and make sure you look sexy."

"Uh, thanks." I exited the office and made my way to my locker, sucking in a deep breath before releasing it into the air. I could do this. I could handle being in the spotlight on my first day.

"You make videos that thousands of people watch, Destiny. You got this," I whispered to myself. After checking my hair and makeup in the bathroom to make sure I still looked okay, I followed the loud noise of people cheering and chanting. My heart started beating profusely when the fighting ring came into view. *Just remember, this is your world now. Get into character.*

My heels clicked the few more feet into the open forum, everything happening in slow motion for a few seconds. The vibe was fire, and I became mesmerized by the men and women filling the seats of the circular seating platform.

"Ah hell," I muttered when I stepped completely into the main fight room. The fighters were making their rounds through the crowd. Each guy had a posse right on his heels, and you could definitely tell the crowd favorites. In that moment, I realized that I hadn't truly prepared myself for this story.

I'd researched fight clubs, mainly illegal ones but a few legal ones as well, and watched a lot of videos. But nothing could have prepared me for being in an actual fight club. The Enclave Fight Club may have been licensed to fight, but the fact still remained if they were illegally gambling on their fighters, and word was, nothing was off limits at Enclave. Looking around at the massive groups of people, I made a mental note to prepare myself if this story took a little longer to solve than I prepped for. *But you've written stories with less time to investigate,* I reminded.

"Are you DK?" asked an attractive girl with a Spanish accent, breaking my thoughts. She was stunning with long, flowing black hair, a tan skin tone, and bright, welcoming eyes. "I'm Selena and I'll be training you this week. Love your look! Are you ready?"

"Umm …" I stammered, something I never did.

"Don't worry," Selena said as she gently touched my arm, "you'll get used to the yelling and testosterone."

Yeah, right. I hadn't paid my way through grad-school with the intention of flaunting my goods in front of half of LA, but that's exactly what I was about to do whether I was ready or not.

"Come on," she said with a laugh. "Let's go." Selena

hopped into the ring and I followed. A man holding a clipboard handed her the microphone.

"Quick, what's your favorite thing to do?" she asked.

I said the first thing that came to mind. "Scuba-diving." I'd recently gotten into the sport, and even though it scared the skit outta me sometimes, I loved every minute of it.

"Are you single?"

"Yes."

"Do you prefer to date girls or guys?"

"Guys."

"What traits do you admire in a man."

Huh? What's with the third degree? Regardless of my confusion, I answered quickly, "Compassion, drive, and understanding. Oh, and it wouldn't hurt if he were fine as hell, too!"

Selena winked. "All right, ladies and gentleman, are you ready for a good night?" she asked to the crowd. In response, they yelled and cheered. She asked them again and the crowd roared even louder.

"That's more like it! Tonight, we have a special introduction to make. She's a bit overwhelmed by our crowd so I want you all to give DK a grand welcome to the Enclave Fight Club team."

The crowd went crazy with applause and lots of male appreciation. I couldn't recall a time in my life when I'd ever felt so welcomed by an audience in person.

"In addition to being drop dead gorgeous, DK is also single. She's looking for a compassionate and understanding man with the drive and courage to do her favorite activity, scuba diving. Sorry, ladies, she's into men only."

It caught me off guard when a few women huffed. "Fellas, you could be the one to steal her heart, so make sure you tip her right on the nights when she's working drinks. And, ladies, don't worry. She seems like a nice girl who likes to get wet, so I'm sure we can bring her around to the dark side."

My eyes flew to Selena as the crowd continued to applaud. Shrugging her shoulders, she passed the mic back to the man with the clipboard. "I'm bi," she explained with a sly smile. "But don't worry, I won't bite. I'm very happy with my fuck buddy right now, so there's no need for me to look elsewhere." She pointed to the good-looking male bartender who gave me a head nod. Suddenly, the entire crowd started going crazy.

"He's here," Selena stated in a huskier voice than before.

"Who's here?" I looked around to follow her line of vision. The crowd started chanting, *"Predator!"* as a guy walked through the aisles wearing all black, his dark hoodie low over his eyes. He had to be a main attraction. It was in his walk. I always felt like a guy's walk said a lot about them and his was giving me all the feels.

Confident, yet approachable. Unhurried, yet prepared. His back was toward me when he removed his hood and waved to the audience. I could tell he was wearing a mask as probably all the fighters did per Steel's rules.

"A fan favorite, huh?"

"Only one of the best street fighters in L.A.," Selena exclaimed. "The fans love to see him, so even though he fights last, Steel makes him walk around before the lower weight fighters get in the ring so that the crowd knows he's here. His fighting skills are lethal, but his looks are even more dangerous."

Slowly, he started to turn toward the ring. I found myself holding my breath in anticipation. When his eyes landed on me, he stopped his perusal of the compact stadium.

"Seems you've caught Predator's attention," Selena whispered in my ear. I wanted to say something back, but I couldn't. His eyes held me hostage and stole my voice. He winked, and I felt my knees get weak under his scrutiny. Selena was right—his looks were deadly in the best way possible.

Unfortunately, I wasn't here to eye fuck his ass on stage. I was here to expose the shit they were doing illegally at Enclave no matter how deep I had to travel into this fucked up rabbit hole to get it. Which meant, this dude—albeit beautiful even with the mask—was a distraction I couldn't afford.

ABOUT THE AUTHOR

Award-winning author, Sherelle Green, is a Chicago native with a dynamic imagination and a passion for reading and writing. To her family and friends, she's known as a hug connoisseur, dishing out as many warm hugs as she can. Reality television and lip gloss may be her guilty pleasures; however, she's in an unapologetic love affair with coffee. On many days, she can be found scouring different shops to add to her coffee mug collection or traveling the world for literary inspiration.

Sherelle loves connecting with readers and other literary enthusiasts. She is one of the founding members of Book Euphoria, a literary group, and Rose Gold Press, a boutique publishing company. She enjoys composing emotionally driven stories that are steamy, edgy, and touch on real life issues. Her overall goal is to create relatable and fierce heroines who are flawed, just like the strong and sexy heroes who fight so hard to win their hearts.

For more information:
www.sherellegreen.com

Made in the USA
Monee, IL
02 April 2020

24290911R00081